Deep-Fried Deception

A Sandy Cove British Mystery
Book 1

Siena Summer

Tomaree Publishing

Copyright © 2024 Siena Summer

All rights reserved.

ISBN paperback 9798320823461

This book is a work of fiction. Names, characters, places and incidents are the product of the author's imagination or are used fictitiously. Any resemblance to actual events, locales, business establishments or persons, living or dead, is entirely coincidental.

This book is licensed for your personal enjoyment only. No part of this publication may be reproduced, stored in a retrieval system, or transmitted in any form or by any means, electronic or mechanical, including photocopying, recording or otherwise, without written permission from the author. Thank you for respecting the hard work of this author.

About the Book

In the idyllic Cornish village of Sandy Cove, Maggie Treloar's life seems picture-perfect. She is the assistant of her aunt's charming shop, 'The Book Nook,' where she indulges in her two passions; reading and baking. Maggie revels in the thrilling world of whodunits, as do all the members of the Mystery Book Club. Her complimentary biscuits are a much-loved feature of 'The Book Nook.' The love of her life, a loveable curly Cavapoo named Biscuit, makes Maggie's life in Sandy Cove complete. **Little did Maggie know she would soon become a character in her own whodunit.**

When one of Maggie's fellow book club members becomes the prime suspect in a murder, her peaceful life takes an unexpected turn. Encouraged by her impulsive cousin and other book club members, Maggie takes it upon herself to venture into amateur sleuthing. With her cousin Kate and Biscuit by her side, Maggie sets out to uncover some clues that could point to the actual murderer. However, as Maggie gets closer to the truth, she begins to overstep the mark, treading dangerously close to getting on the wrong side of the law.

Can she work out who the real killer is and clear her friend's name? Can she stay on the right side of the law?

The Sandy Cove British Mystery Series

Prequel Novella: Puppy Farm Peril

(available now)

Short Story: The Bewildering Book Burglary

(coming soon)

Book One: Deep-Fried Deception

(available now)

Book Two: Vanishing Vows

(pre-order now)

Book Three: Murder and Mistletoe

-a Christmas novella

(available October 2024)

Dedication

For all those, like me,
who love to curl up with a good, cosy mystery.

A Note to the Reader

I AM THRILLED TO welcome you to the world of my first fiction series. Yes, there will be more books coming soon. I'm already in different stages of writing the first few books in this series.

In this book, the story takes place in the fictional village of Sandy Cove, situated in Cornwall, Britain. In keeping with the authentic experience, you'll notice that the story follows British spelling, grammar and turns of phrase. This intentional choice aims to immerse you fully in the atmosphere and language of the setting, allowing you to feel the nuances of the characters and their surroundings.

Thank you for embarking on this literary adventure with me. I sincerely hope you enjoy the journey.

Siena Summer

Chapter One

"FOR THE LAST TIME, *no*."

"I'm giving you a reasonable offer, Mrs Edwards."

Maggie heard the voices from within as she pushed open the door to the bookshop, the familiar sound of the little antique bell ringing above her head. Her arms were filled with boxes of biscuits, and one hand gripped a lead, so she was forced to nudge the door open with her back.

"Reasonable? You call that offer reasonable? Then you must be mad," Aunt June said with a raised voice.

"You aren't going to get a better deal than–"

"Lucky for me, I don't want a deal in the first place because, as I've been telling you for the past two years... I'm. Not. Selling."

Maggie turned around to see her Aunt June on the other side of the counter, arms folded. Her aunt's blue eyes blazed as she glared at the man in the shop. He was facing away from Maggie, so all she could see was the tall build and thinning brown hair. But she didn't need to see the man's face to recognise his voice. And even if she hadn't recognised his voice, there was only one man in the village who could annoy June this much.

"Good morning, Mr Larkin," Maggie said.

Joseph Larkin turned, glancing at Maggie before turning back and disregarding her entirely.

"Mrs Edwards," Larkin said, his voice nasally and condescending. "You really need to consider the times. People aren't coming to bookshops anymore. They're buying everything online and reading on their tablet. You are obsolete."

June stared at him. If looks could kill, Larkin wouldn't quite be dead, but certainly maimed.

"Our sales numbers would beg to differ," Maggie said a bit tersely as she carried the biscuits over to the counter. She put herself between her aunt and Larkin, making it very clear he would have to deal with her if he said anything else. Meanwhile, Maggie's dog, Biscuit, completely oblivious to the fact that June was fuming, trotted over to Larkin and began sniffing him. She let out a low growl, then ran back to Maggie. Larkin frowned at her before turning his attention back to June.

"I'll give you time to think it over, then," Larkin said. Without another word, as though dismissing the two of them entirely from his mind, he turned and casually sauntered out of The Book Nook, as though he'd been searching for a novel and hadn't found it, rather than attempting to convince June to sell her beloved bookshop.

"Are you all right?" Maggie asked, opening the first box of biscuits so she could transfer them to a glass jar. "I...Biscuit, no!"

Her beautiful, sometimes infuriating, Cavapoo had jumped up, placing her front paws on the counter as she lunged for the nearest biscuit. She whined when Maggie nudged her gently to the ground, then plodded off, staying within sprinting distance in case Maggie accidentally dropped any of her favourite treats.

"I'm fine," June said, in a tone that meant she was anything but. "That man has been hounding me for two years. When is he going to get the hint that even if I want to sell, it won't be to him?"

"Probably never," Maggie said, putting the lid back on the jar.

June shook her head, exasperated. She grabbed a large box of books hauled them over to one side and began sorting. Maggie recognised the behaviour; she'd seen her aunt 'angry organise' often enough to know that was exactly what she was doing. "At best that's half what the building's worth, and that doesn't even include the business itself. Can you believe that?"

"From him? Absolutely."

Joseph Larkin was notorious around town for snapping up land for incredibly low prices, then building cheap tourist attractions and souvenir shops in their place. He and his wife had lived in a large Georgian manor in Sandy Cove for the last decade, but the residents of Sandy Cove still didn't trust him or see him as a local. Joseph Larkin travelled to London a lot for work, but he always summered at Sandy Cove. There were maybe a handful of people in town who had anything nice to say about him. Maggie was not one of them, nor was June.

"I heard he's planning on building a hotel or resort," Maggie said. She walked over to her aunt and picked up a stack of books, carrying them over to their rightful shelf. "He's probably making similar offers to everyone on this block."

"Lucky me," June said.

Maggie stopped and placed her handful of books back on the floor, and went over to her aunt.

"Seriously, are you okay?" she asked.

June took a deep breath, then brushed strands of her brown hair from her face. At that moment, her aunt looked incredibly tired. Her blue eyes, which were usually so bright, had dulled. And though she normally looked incredibly youthful for her age, that morning she was showing every bit of her 58 years. "Just annoyed," she said. "I don't particularly like it when pompous city men like Larkin call my business 'obsolete.'"

Maggie gave her a side hug. "You know he just said that to get under your skin," she said. "And besides, we know it's not true."

The Book Nook was nestled in the heart of the village of Sandy Cove and had proven very popular ever since June first opened its doors, and for good reason. It had a vast selection of books, of course. June's passion was for fiction, evidenced by a collection that ranged from Victorian classics to the latest bestsellers. But that's not to forget the shelves that journeyed through all periods of history, the collection of quirky cookbooks, and the array of biographies that covered pretty much anyone a customer could ask for. But when June had envisioned her shop, she had pictured it as a cosy place for people to read, discover and purchase new and pre-loved books. She wanted to share her deep love of books with anyone who stepped through the door.

Everything in the shop had June's personal touch to it. The gentle chime of a small brass bell tinkling above the door would signal the arrival of a new customer or an old regular, a sound that had always brought her joy. The shop was as warm and inviting as the greeting you would receive from June, Maggie, and Biscuit. The air was filled with the rich aroma of freshly brewed tea and homemade biscuits, and the smell of books seemed to have soaked into the building. The inviting atmosphere beckoned visitors to explore the literary treasures within.

The sunlight filtering through the glass window cast a warm and inviting glow upon the space. The natural light breathed life into the bookshop, gently illuminating the rows of rustic bookshelves filled to the brim with volumes of all shapes and sizes. Each shelf was a treasure trove, home to books of various genres, their spines beckoning with tantalising titles and vibrant covers.

There were plush chairs scattered throughout the shop, their upholstery worn with love and countless hours of reading. The chairs were strategically placed, offering quiet corners and cosy nooks, perfect for solitary immersion into the pages of a beloved novel. The seats were soft and plush, providing comfort and support as though they had been designed with the sole purpose of allowing avid readers to sit for ages as their imaginations roamed the pages of their books. Beside the chairs were little tables where you could place a complimentary cup of tea and a biscuit while you scanned the pages of your books. Everything in The Book Nook had been meticulously planned, every aspect designed with the sole purpose of allowing people to enjoy books at their leisure, regardless of whether they purchased them or not.

Every bit of effort June had put into the business had paid off. June had spent years of her life pouring love into her business. It was a thriving, popular bookshop that locals and tourists loved, regardless of what men like Larkin said.

"It doesn't make it any less frustrating," June said. "And you know, I heard from Liv that he's been harassing Sam again. Apparently, he's been snooping around trying to find an excuse to have him shut down."

"I'm not surprised," Maggie said. "Hasn't he done that before?"

June nodded, running her fingers through her hair. "Once or twice, at least," she said. "But Sam's smart and knows how to get Larkin off his back, otherwise Sam would have been shut down ages ago."

"And I know for a fact that you can hold your own against Larkin just as much as Sam can," Maggie said. "But talking about Sam is making me think about food. Would you want to go out for a long lunch? We could walk along the beach and grab some fish and chips at his restaurant. I've been craving some for ages."

June eyed her in an *I know what you're doing* sort of way. June wasn't stupid, and Maggie knew her aunt was aware of exactly what she was trying to do. But she relented.

"That sounds really nice, actually," she said. "Anything to get my mind off Joseph Larkin. But first, I want to finish shelving these books."

The door chimed cheerily, the way it always did when someone walked in. The two women turned to see a middle-aged couple looking around the shop.

"Good morning," the woman said. "I was hoping you might have some fun beach reads. I forgot to pack mine."

Maggie stood, smiling.

"I think I've got just the thing," she said. "Why don't you follow me?"

~~~

Sandy Cove was a picturesque seaside village in Cornwall, known for its pristine cerulean water, sandy beaches, and majestic cliffs encircling the area. It was the type of place where almost everyone knew each other. Its harbour drew people like a magnet, and tourists flocked to the village in summer, nearly doubling its population.

Everywhere you went you could smell the sea, and the air was filled with the sound of gulls. The narrow, cobbled streets wound their way between rows of painted stone cottages. Each dwelling was adorned with brightly coloured doors and window boxes bursting with vibrant blooms. They exuded an irresistible charm. Many of the original fishermen's cottages were now quaint little shops containing homemade crafts, art galleries, cosy tea rooms, pubs, and restaurants. Further back, beginning to creep up the edge of the cliffs, were a handful of hotels and houses. About a five-minute drive from town was a small surfing point known mostly to locals, where they could get far better waves than inside the enclosed harbour. Maggie felt that the cosiness and warmth that June had so lovingly instilled in The Book Nook had spread out into the streets of the village around it.

When lunchtime came around, June put a handwritten sign in the window saying they were closed for lunch,

The Book Nook was close enough to the sea to smell the salt water when Maggie and June emerged from the building and made their way towards the beach, with Biscuit tugging excitedly at her lead. They strolled along the winding streets, looking in the windows of the shops they passed by. They waved to the locals they passed, stopping periodically for Biscuit to receive her regular attention and fussing from people they passed.

Once they reached the soft sand, Maggie kicked off her shoes. She looked out at the beautiful crystalline water dotted with colourful fishing boats and listened to the sounds of a beach alive with the cries of delighted children playing in the sand.

"You're going to burn your feet," June said.

"I can always put them back on," Maggie pointed out, smiling. She took a deep breath, relishing the scent and feel of the sea air. The midday sun beat down pleasantly, and the wind whipped her auburn hair back behind her. Out here, the unpleasantness of Joseph Larkin had swept away with the outgoing tide.

"It's gorgeous outside," Maggie said.

June nodded her agreement, but her eyes were still far away, her shoulders tense with lingering irritation.

"You can't let him get to you," Maggie said. "There's nothing he can do beyond annoy you."

"But what if he tries to shut me down?" she asked. "He's done it to other businesses."

"Then we'll stop him. Trust me, we aren't going to let him run you out of business." When June still didn't look at ease, Maggie leaned in closer. "And we can always sue him for harassment. He'll have a lot more on his mind than pestering you if we do that."

June laughed, and the tension in her shoulders eased. Maggie smiled. She hated the idea of June being upset. She had always been more or less a second mother to Maggie for most of her life.

Even when Maggie had lived in London, she and her aunt would talk weekly, catching up and checking in on one another. And when Maggie had decided to leave London rather abruptly, June had offered her a job at The Book Nook. She owed a lot to her aunt, and the least she could do was make her smile on occasion.

The three of them walked along the beach, Biscuit periodically darting into the water excitedly before running back to the women, shaking her curly, ruby-coloured fur and sending sea water along their legs and shirts. They passed shops and restaurants that lined the beach, their colourful fronts on display to everyone who walked along the sand. These included the surfing shop where all the locals bought their gear, and Abigail's bakery, which was called Sweet Treats on Seaview Street. Then there was The Smuggler's Inn, Maggie's favourite pub, as well as several kitschy shops and quirky cafes that tourists could not keep themselves away from.

As they walked, Maggie turned and glanced up the cliffs. The Larkin Manor, an old Georgian mansion, was visible from here as it looked out on the ocean. It was a beautiful manor, one that Maggie had admired nearly her whole life, even if she had never been able to see it up close. The fact that it belonged to a man like Larkin seemed unfair.

"There are lots of fishing boats out today, said Maggie, pointing out towards the water, where several colourful boats–too far away to be distinguished properly–dotted the ocean. "Hopefully the fishing trawlers left them some fish. Is Uncle Jim out there?"

June laughed. "It's a Saturday in the summer," she said. "Of course, he is. But if he isn't out at Surfer's Point by this afternoon, I'll eat my signed copy of *The Stand*, page by page."

"What, not *The Fellowship of the Ring* or *Rebecca*?"

June looked at her askance. "Please," she said. "I'd bet my own life before I risked those. I have two Stephen King books. I can afford to lose one."

They laughed as they continued down the beach, weaving through the throng of locals and tourists. It was a Saturday and packed as usual. The soles of Maggie's feet were indeed beginning to get a little hot, but she wasn't about to give June the satisfaction of being able to say *I told you so*, so she didn't say anything. Besides, their destination was in sight. A blue and white building with a large terrace facing the ocean grew ever closer.

"This was a good idea, Maggie," June said. "Thanks. I needed this."

"Of course," Maggie said, giving her aunt another side hug. "I'm always here for you."

There was a slightly indignant-sounding *woof!* Maggie and June looked down to see Biscuit peering up at them, her soulful brown eyes looking almost wounded.

"Biscuit is too, of course," Maggie added.

The Cavapoo's tail wagged excitedly, and before Maggie or June could say anything else, Biscuit was tugging excitedly on her lead, desperate to pull them up the steps to Sam's restaurant, "The Lively Catch."

Chapter Two

SAM'S RESTAURANT HAD BEEN a staple of Sandy Cove for as long as Maggie could remember. Maggie had been coming here since she was a kid. She had no idea what Sam and his cook did to make the chips so crisp, or the fish so perfectly battered, but she swore there was something addictive about them.

As Maggie, June and Biscuit entered the local 'chippy,' The Lively Catch, the aroma of freshly fried fish and chips greeted them. Perched on the edge of the sandy shoreline, the restaurant boasted a lively atmosphere, with a cheerful buzz of conversation and the ever-constant clinking of cutlery. Inside, the restaurant was cosy and welcoming, and the wooden interior was painted to look worn and salt-stained. It was tastefully decorated with charming maritime objects scattered throughout the restaurant. The large windows allowed the natural light to flood in, further adding to the cheerful atmosphere. It was the perfect mix of Sam and his wife Liv.

Behind the counter, the bustling kitchen crew were busy frying up fresh catches from local fishermen, caught with expertise and precision. The menu was displayed on blackboards and featured classic fish and chips, but also succulent scampi, tender calamari rings and flaky cod.

The restaurant was busy, and Maggie hoped that there would be a table available out on the terrace.

"Hey, Maggie! Hi, Mrs Edwards," said Elle, one of Sam's long-term waitresses.

"The place is certainly busy today," said Maggie, "it looks like everyone is craving Sam's fish and chips."

"That's for sure, said Elle. We are always run off our feet in the summer, but we'll always make room for our regulars," Elle said cheerily as she led them out on the terrace. "I'll get you some drinks," said Elle, "and tell Sam you're here."

The restaurant's terrace was draped with umbrellas, and it offered an unobstructed view of Sandy Cove beach and harbour. There were wooden tables with nautical-themed décor which invited the diners to sit back and enjoy their meals while soaking in the breathtaking coastal panorama. Their table was in the corner of the terrace, where the sea breeze drifted pleasantly towards them.

A few minutes later, a man in his mid-fifties walked up, grinning broadly. His brown hair had a smattering of grey and currently had flecks of sand throughout. It had dried in stringy clumps, indicative of hair that had recently been immersed in seawater.

"Hey, you two," Sam said, his eyes crinkling. He bent down to pet Biscuit. "I didn't know you were coming by today."

"Last minute emergency that required comfort food," Maggie said. "Were you surfing this morning?"

"What gave it away?" he asked. "The sand in my hair or the fact that I smell like seawater?"

"Mostly the fact that Biscuit is trying to lick you." Maggie laughed as Biscuit, tail wagging so enthusiastically her rear was joining in, licked eagerly at Sam's hand. "She does that whenever I come out of the ocean. I think it's the salt."

Grinning, Sam crouched down and scratched both sides of Biscuit's neck, who took this opportunity to lick his face.

"Oh, have you finished the new book yet, Sam?" June asked eagerly. "I can't wait to talk about it!"

Sam, Maggie, June, as well as five others, were all part of the 'Mystery Book Club', or MBC for short. They met once a month at The Book Nook, talking about whatever book they were reading for over an hour before conversation naturally drifted to different topics. June had created it a handful of years earlier when she was horrified to discover that her friends, Helena and Liv, had never read an Agatha Christie novel. She created the book group immediately, which only later came to be known as the MBC. The name had come about organically after they realised that the majority of books they read were mysteries. Maggie had joined when she moved back from London, which brought their member count to eight.

Sam gave a sheepish, almost guilty expression. "Not yet," he said. "I've been a bit busy."

"How far have you got?" Maggie asked, already guessing the answer.

"Er..." he coughed. "Well, the murder's happened."

Maggie lapsed into giggles while June gave Sam a horrified look.

"That's twenty pages in!" she said.

"I know," he said. "Don't worry, I'll have it finished in time."

"The meeting is Wednesday evening," June said.

"I know," he said, and grinned. "That means I'll have all day Wednesday to read it. Plenty of time."

Maggie laughed again while June shook her head in exasperation. "You better," she said. "Or I'll make sure Maggie forgets to bake your favourite Victoria sponge cake."

"We can't have that, can we? In that case, I'll be sure to start on Tuesday." Before June could open her mouth to dish out another scolding, he asked, "The usual?"

"You know us too well," Maggie answered. "And don't worry, your sponge cake is safe."

"Well, that's a relief. Let me clean up." Sam stood, brushing off his trousers. "Most people don't like dog slobber in their food. I'll go ahead and put your order in."

"Better make that three, mate." Another slightly older man came up, clapping Sam companionably on the back. "Or four. I'm starving. Mind if I sit down, ladies?"

"Not at all," June said.

Bert Williams, another member of the MBC, was tall and had aged in such a way that made one think he was a decade younger than his actual 61. His hair still had streaks of blonde running through it and was as thick as a twenty-year-old's, with no signs of balding anywhere to be seen. He gave his trademark relaxed smile as he settled himself in the chair.

"I'll start you with one," Sam said. "If you're still hungry after that, I'll get you another. I'd rather you not eat all my food if you can help it."

"No promises. It's pretty tasty."

Sam made a mock grimace before wandering back towards the kitchen.

"How are you doing?" June asked.

"Can't complain," Bert said. The waitress brought their drinks, and Bert took a big gulp of his pint of local ale. "Things have been a bit dull, but besides that, things have been all right. What about you ladies? Book Nook keeping you busy?"

"Always," June said, then sniffed. "Though some people would beg to disagree."

Bert looked from June's annoyed expression to Maggie's sympathetic one. His brown eyes studied them in confusion.

"What am I missing?" he asked.

"Oh, just Joseph Larkin trying to push June into selling the shop," Maggie said, rolling her eyes. "He was there this morning."

"Oh, him." Bert tutted. "He's back in town? I hoped we'd have a few more weeks at least before we had to deal with his charming personality again. Really, I don't get why he keeps coming back, since no one here likes him."

"From what I can tell, it's his wife," June said. "She stays here year-round and he goes off and does whatever he pleases until summer, when he comes back."

"You'd think he'd have the decency to stay here all the time if he's so bent on buying up land," Bert said. "But some people have got no taste. At least when George Evans buys up property, he puts money back into the community."

Maggie was about to answer when a loud voice cut through the quiet din of lively conversations like a sledgehammer.

"Can you believe this place, Amélie? It's filthy."

"Speak of the devil," Bert said. "There goes my 'Days Not Having to Listen to a Git' streak."

Maggie glanced up to see Joseph Larkin, still in his suit and tie, sitting down at a nearby table. The man looked completely out of place amongst the casually dressed tourists in shorts and sandals. The sun beating down emphasised the bald spot that had long been widening at the back of his scalp.

The woman with him was Amélie Larkin, his wife, and she looked absolutely stunning. The designer clothes were in a beach style that fit in far more with her surroundings than her husband's stuffy suit, and clung perfectly to her slender frame. Her dark hair cascaded down to her shoulders. Her eyes were hidden behind dark sunglasses even as her head was angled down to look at her phone.

June's jaw had clenched so tightly that Maggie couldn't have pried open her mouth with a crowbar.

"We can go somewhere else," Maggie whispered.

June shook her head, fire blazing in her blue eyes.

"No," she said. "I'm not letting him ruin my lunch as well as my morning."

"Good on you, June," Bert said. "Don't give him any power over you."

By the expressions of the people around them and the general hush in conversation, their table wasn't the only one annoyed by Larkin's outburst. And he was still going.

"I mean, look at it. Sand all over the place, sticky tables and menus. I don't even want to think about what the kitchen must look like."

"Then don't eat here, you prat," Bert said, not quite loud enough to carry past their table. "Seriously, why come here if all you want to do is complain? And why the ruddy hell is he shouting so everyone can hear him?"

"That's the point," Maggie said. "I know exactly what he's doing."

"Could the service be any slower?" Larkin yelled. Beside him, Mrs Larkin seemed disengaged, staring at her phone and effectively tuning her husband out. "I'm going to grow old and die waiting to order."

June gave an expression that very much indicated she wouldn't have a problem with that but kept her mouth shut. Biscuit whimpered and put her head in June's lap, looking up at her with soulful eyes, her tail wagging gently. June's features softened and she scratched the dog behind the ears.

"Thanks, girl," June said.

"*Finally*," Larkin announced as a young girl stepped timidly up to the table. He was still yelling loudly enough that sunbathers could probably hear him on the beach. "We've been waiting for ages. My wife is starving."

"Yes dear," Mrs Larkin said at a far more reasonable decibel. She didn't look up from her phone. "That's right."

"What is he doing, then?" Bert asked, watching the exchange from out of the corner of his eye. "If he harasses that poor girl anymore, I'm going to go over and have a nice little chat with him."

"He's trying to make people leave," Maggie suggested. "Or prevent more people from coming." 'He's trying to drive customers away," she said. "You know that rash of bad reviews Sam got a couple of months back that he ended up proving were false? I'd bet my hat that was Larkin and his friends. The fewer people come to Sam's restaurant, the more likely it is he'll be forced to sell."

"So it doesn't matter if he makes himself look like an idiot" Bert said, still watching. "He stirs up trouble, and Sam has to deal with the aftermath."

"That's my theory, at least," Maggie said. "I wouldn't be surprised if he's done the same thing at other places he wants to get his hands on."

"Solid theory, if you ask me," June said. "I know he's been able to sue a couple of places, force them into bankruptcy, then snatch up the property as soon as they sold."

"Well, he's got another thing coming if he thinks that's going to work here," Bert said. "I can't imagine Liv taking that lying down, can you?"

"Not a chance," Maggie said. Liv might seem like the friendly hairdresser hungry for gossip (which she unquestionably was), but she was also terrifying if you got on her bad side.

The waitress had scurried away to the kitchen, leaving Larkin and his wife alone. Larkin dropped to a quieter volume, though still speaking loudly enough for anyone who wanted to eavesdrop to do so. He was keeping up his half of a very one-sided conversation, his voice just so happening to rise whenever he dropped in another insult about the establishment. His wife continued to seem completely disengaged from the conversation, though that didn't seem to faze him in the least.

After a couple of minutes, however, Joseph Larkin became background noise. Maggie, Bert, and June had a pleasant conversation, talking about everything but the couple a few tables over from them. By the time their fish and chips had arrived, they had almost entirely blocked the unpleasant man from their mind.

The fish and chips were piping hot and smelled tantalisingly delicious. Maggie's stomach rumbled, and she began eating enthusiastically. Occasionally she would give in to Biscuit's pleading gaze and give her a bit of fish without the batter, which the cute Cavapoo relished.

"I don't know what he does, but I swear the man must put something addictive in the batter," Bert said before popping a piece of fish into his mouth. "I've asked him a hundred times for his recipe and he's never told me what it is."

"That's because he knows you'll tell everyone you possibly can as soon as you figure it out," June said.

"I can't help it if I can't keep a secret."

"I'm fairly certain that you can. Isn't that the whole point of a secret?"

A loud cry of "It's about time!" came from the direction of Joseph Larkin's table. Maggie rolled her eyes. They must have gotten their food.

June took another bite of the fish and frowned, her brow furrowing in confusion.

"Does the fish taste different to either of you?" she asked.

Maggie chewed another piece, her head leaning to one side as she tried to focus on the taste.

"Now that you mention it," she said. "I think you may be right. I can't tell what it is, though."

She tasted it again. It did taste different—but it was subtle. It was almost, perhaps... earthier? But that wasn't right. She recognised the taste. It was on the tip of her tongue.

A scream pierced through her thoughts. Maggie jumped, spinning around wildly to see what was wrong. A moment later, choking, gasping sounds began growing louder, as did cries of alarm.

Her eyes found the Larkins' table and stayed glued there.

Joseph Larkin was on the ground, scratching desperately at his throat. Someone—a sunburned tourist in capri shorts and boat shoes—ran over and crouched next to him, to see if he could help.

"I'll go for Dr Remington," Elle said, tossing her empty tray on a table before darting down the wooden stairs and out of site.

Amélie was rummaging frantically in her purse. Her sunglasses had slipped and were hanging from one earlobe, but she didn't seem to notice.

"It's not here," she said, her voice panicked and confused. "I can't find it."

She turned her purse upside down and shook it violently. A compact, a tube of lipstick, and a loose credit card, along with the rest of the bag's contents, fell to the ground.

"Does anyone have an EpiPen?" she screamed. "Anyone?"

But everyone remained still as stone, all watching in horror.

No one had called 999. Maggie hurriedly dug in her pocket for her phone and pulled it out, hastily punching in the numbers. She put the phone to her ear.

"999, what's your emergency?" said the woman on the other end.

"Yes, hi, I'm in Sandy Cove at The Lively Catch Restaurant. You need to call an ambulance. There's a man—he's having trouble breathing."

"Okay, now tell me, is—"

But Maggie barely heard as a grave hush fell over the crowd. Maggie glanced over and could see instantly why.

"Never mind," she said. "I think he's dead."

Chapter Three

AMÉLIE LARKIN'S SCREAM OF horror pierced the air and Maggie's eardrums. She winced, her phone still to her ear.

"Okay," the operator said, "I need you to stay on the line."

By now, several people from the beach had come running, mostly to stare at the scene unfolding before their eyes. A few surprised gasps and cries came from the growing crowd. Sam had rushed from the restaurant's interior and pushed his way to the front, his face as pale as a ghost's. Bert had run up too, trying to see if there was any way he could help.

"Excuse me, police, excu—thank you. Police, everyone, please get out of the way."

An attractive, dark-haired man in a wetsuit pushed his way through the crowd. He pushed his still-damp hair from his eyes as he scanned the crowd. Maggie knew him, as he had replaced her Uncle Jim as detective inspector of the local police station, when he had retired.

"Everyone, please back up a few steps!" Detective Inspector Tom Pearce called. "Thank you." His voice was strong and authoritative, the kind that people listened to without thinking. "Has anyone called 999?" he asked. "Or gone to fetch the doctor?"

"I have 999 on the phone," Maggie said, holding her phone in the air.

DI Pearce's dark eyes found hers and blinked with recognition, before he walked purposefully towards her, hand outstretched.

"May I?" he asked.

She handed him the phone. "One of the waitresses has gone to get the doctor," she added. DI Pearce nodded before stepping away from her and back to where Larkin was lying on the floor, nudging people gently out of the way.

Maggie took a moment, as the shock wore off, to look around the crowd. Amélie Larkin was standing next to their table, her mouth open in horror as she looked down at her husband. She wasn't crying; she just looked stunned. For some reason, the lack of tears didn't surprise Maggie in the slightest. A tourist was kneeling down over Joseph Larkin performing CPR and a crowd of onlookers was gathering on the beach. Maggie looked over at her Aunt June, who looked just as worried and shocked as everyone else. Maggie was concerned for her aunt and how she would be feeling about what had occurred. Although her aunt disliked Joseph Larkin, she would never have wished for this to happen.

"Junie?" Maggie jumped when another familiar figure—in swimming trunks, a T-shirt, and a fisherman's cap—pushed through the crowd and approached them. Her Uncle Jim put one hand on June's shoulder. "I'd just docked and was walking over here to say hi to Sam when I heard the screams. What happened?"

"I don't know," June said, still in shock. "One minute, he was fine; the next, he was on the ground choking."

"I don't think it was choking, I think it was an allergic reaction," Maggie said. "Remember his wife talking about an EpiPen?"

June and Jim glanced over at her, mildly surprised. She shrugged. Biscuit was at her heels, whimpering softly as the chaos unfolded around them. Sam and Bert came over to join them after a minute.

"You all right, Sam?" Jim asked. Uncle Jim was calm and collected, despite the chaos. Being a retired detective probably helped with that.

"As well as I can be when a man keels over in your restaurant," Sam answered. Jim gave a *that's fair* bob of the head, then opened his mouth to ask something else. But the sound of pounding footsteps charging up the wooden steps cut him off. Detective Inspector Pearce waved an older, grey-haired man over to the body. Dr Remington had been the village doctor for nearly 30 years. He then quickly walked towards Maggie, her phone in his hand.

"Do you mind if I make a couple more calls? My phone is in my car, and I'd rather not leave the scene."

"Of course," she said.

He nodded. Even in a wetsuit, there was nothing but professionalism in his stance and expression. Regardless of what he had been doing earlier, he was on the job now, and nothing was going to stop that. It was rather admirable.

"Appreciate it. I'll be right back." He stepped away, tapping quickly on the screen of Maggie's phone. Maggie took the time to observe Dr Remington. He had already jabbed an EpiPen into Larkin's leg, but it didn't seem to have any effect. A minute later, he told the tourist who had been doing the chest compressions that there was no need to continue.

DI Pearce came back with her phone, tearing her gaze away from the body.

"Here you go," he said. "Sorry, I might have got a bit of salt water on it. I wasn't exactly expecting to be on duty today. I was driving back from Surfer's Point and I heard the scream as I drove by."

"You mean this isn't official police attire?" Maggie asked in mock surprise. "For a moment I thought they had changed the uniform."

DI Pearce gave a soft chuckle as Maggie took back the phone. "Maybe in a few years they will, if I'm lucky." He quietened his voice a little. "So, did you see what happened?"

She sighed. She had a funny feeling this was going to be a recurring question over the next few days, if not the next few weeks.

"We were eating over here when we heard a scream," she said. "We looked up to see Joseph Larkin on the ground. He wasn't responding to anyone's help, and his wife said something about an EpiPen."

"She thinks it was an allergic reaction," Bert said, jabbing his thumb at Maggie. She gave him an irritated look as she tried to hide her discomfort at being singled out. "What? You did," he said.

The inspector raised an eyebrow and looked at her. She shrugged, suddenly self-conscious. "Like I said, his wife was looking for an EpiPen. There's only one reason she'd be doing that while her husband is rasping on the ground next to her."

He nodded, his gaze glassy as if he were lost in thought. "Well, the ambulance will be here soon enough to take the body to the morgue, but they're over in Winfeld. So, ah—"

DI Pearce cut himself off as a young man in a constable's uniform trotted up to him.

"Sorry, it took me a while, sir," the man said.

"It hasn't even been ten minutes since I called you, Matthew," the inspector said. "You're fine."

"What happened?" Matthew asked. His blue eyes were bright with interest. It wasn't hard to see that he was forcing himself not to bounce on the balls of his feet.

"Most likely an accident," DI Pearce replied. He turned to Maggie and the others, gesturing at the newcomer. "This is our new constable, Matthew Brown."

"Pleasure," said Jim. Bert grunted, which was about as friendly as he got when it came to officers.

DI Pearce turned toward Constable Brown. "Right now, if you wouldn't mind getting everyone off the terrace that would be a great help. This area needs to be cordoned off."

"Yes, sir."

But before the young man could go about his task, Biscuit rushed forward, tearing her lead out of Maggie's loose grip. She lolloped towards Matthew, her tail and backside wagging excitedly. She shoved her nose against the constable's pocket and made an excited chuffing sound.

"Oh, no, I'm so sorry." Maggie moved forward to grab Biscuit's lead and pull her back. "Biscuit, no."

Constable Brown's eyes lit up with boyish excitement. "Hello there, girl," he said, scratching her head. "Aren't you a cutie."

Maggie tugged at the lead, but Biscuit wouldn't budge. Instead, she made a soft keening sound as she stared longingly at the constable's pocket. Maggie understood immediately.

"You don't happen to have any biscuits in there, do you?" she asked.

He turned bright red and pulled out a small ziplock bag from the pocket Biscuit had been so thoroughly investigating. She immediately sat right in front of him, her eyes glued to the bag as she licked her chops.

"DI Pearce called right when I was about to have lunch," he said. "I had to run over from the station."

Biscuit whined again, shifting on her feet and looking at Matthew with adoring eyes. Maggie sighed and gave up trying to pull her away.

"I'm so sorry," she said. "I swear she has a radar in her head that tells her where the nearest biscuits are."

"Either that or she's just got a good nose, don't you, girl?" He spoke in a baby voice to Biscuit, scratching her head again. Then, in a normal voice, he added, "Do you mind if I give her one? I don't mind sharing with such a sweetie."

"If you want to, but she may never leave you alone ever again."

He handed the Cavapoo a biscuit, which promptly vanished. The dog licked the constable's hand appreciatively. Satisfied now that her tithe had been paid, she padded back to the rest of the group with Maggie.

DI Pearce had been watching the entire thing with bemused interest. Finally, he said, "Constable Brown, the crowd?"

"Oh." Matthew turned bright red and looked around at everyone as if only now registering the large number of people awkwardly standing about, looking at the corpse or at the detectives, muttering in small clusters. "Right. Sorry, sir."

"And make sure none of them are taking photos," the inspector added. He glanced over at the small group and gave an apologetic smile. "I'm afraid that means you lot as well. But stick around, if you wouldn't mind."

Bert opened his mouth as if about to protest, but Jim said, "That's fine, Tom, thanks a bunch," and ushered the group down the steps onto the beach.

"Don't forget you're retired, Jim," Bert said, grumbling.

"He's just doing his job. No need to get sulky," Jim said.

They joined the rest of the throng on the beach, waiting patiently to be allowed to leave. Sam seemed pale and looked sick to his stomach, his eyes constantly darting up to the terrace where the new widow and the police were talking. She could understand why. If there had been something wrong with his food that had resulted in Larkin's death, he could be ruined or end up in prison.

Maggie shifted from foot to foot. She couldn't see the body from this angle, but she could see the top of Dr Remington's head as he hunched over it. At that moment, she wanted nothing more than to hear what was going on. She had just seen a man die. She was in shock, certainly, still processing what had just happened. But that didn't change the fact that she wanted to know why someone was dead.

"Come on, Biscuit," Maggie said. "Looks like you might need to go to the loo again."

The two of them walked close to the terrace, keeping a low profile and trying to stay relatively out of sight. They moved to where they were almost entirely beneath it. Maggie listened as Biscuit sniffed eagerly at the sand.

"You're sure?" the Inspector was asking.

"I've been a doctor for over thirty years, Detective Inspector. I know an allergic reaction when I see one," Dr Remington replied.

"I told you so," a woman's voice said, her voice crisp and incredibly derogatory. "You didn't need a doctor to tell you that."

"I know, Mrs Larkin," DI Pearce said patiently. "But we needed a professional's opinion as well."

"Well, you've got it," Dr Remington said.

"Any way of telling what allergy it was?" he asked.

"I've treated him in the past. He only had the one: peanuts," Remington said.

Maggie's brow furrowed as the words sunk in. *Peanuts?* She was certain she'd heard him right, but something about it struck her as very odd.

"Excuse me, Miss Treloar?"

She jumped at the voice and looked up. Detective Inspector Pearce was leaning over the wooden railing, looking down at her with a knowing smirk. "When you're done walking Biscuit, would you mind asking your friend, Mr Murphy—Sam—to come see me?"

She smiled innocently, feeling herself turning red. "Sorry, Detective Inspector," she said. "I think your constable must have dropped a biscuit down here. She was so insistent we come this way."

"I'll be sure to tell Matthew to keep a closer eye on his food, then."

She walked back to her group, pondering over the scant amount of information she'd gathered.

"The detective inspector wants to see you, Sam," Maggie said.

"Figured he might." He sighed. "Well, let's get this over with."

He had taken two steps when she stopped him. "Do you use peanuts in anything you cook, by any chance?" she asked.

He didn't even have to think.

"Of course not," he said. "No reason to."

Then he trotted back up the stairs towards the detective, leaving Maggie with a burning question.

When had Joseph Larkin had the time to eat peanuts while in Sam's restaurant?

Chapter Four

"I NEVER LIKED THAT man," Liv declared. "If you'd heard half the stories I have about him..."

"We have, Liv," Bert said, grinning. "You spread every story that comes through that salon of yours."

"Then you know what a horrid man he is." Liv caught a glimpse of her reflection in the display case and fixed a stray hair.

"I can't believe that the one weekend I go to Exeter, a man dies while you're out at lunch," Kate said. Kate was June's daughter, and she and Maggie were as close as siblings. Both girls were in their twenties, with Maggie being a few years older. They had grown up together in Sandy Cove. Kate's long blonde hair was tied up in a high ponytail, and she was dressed in her usual Bohemian attire. She had a bubbly, infectious personality and was prone to spontaneity.

"I mean, don't get me wrong," said Kate, "it's horrid that it happened, but it would have been fascinating to see."

It was Wednesday evening, the bookshop was closed and all eight members of the MBC had gathered in The Book Nook. Some armchairs and chairs were arranged in a circle around a table. Two half-empty teapots, decorated in tea cosies knitted to look like cute, chubby Jane Austen characters, lay on the table, along with a Victoria sponge cake and a tray of Maggie's biscuits. This evening's selection included Cornish fairings – a spiced ginger biscuit, shortbread and homemade wagon wheels – a sandwich biscuit filled with jam and marshmallow and covered in chocolate. A large portion of these treats had already gone. Biscuit had already enjoyed a shortbread and was now curled up, sleeping in an armchair with her favourite bunny toy. The MBC's copies of this month's book—*Broken Harbour* by Tana French—lay at their feet, or in their laps, as they had finished their discussion of the book and had now moved on to discussing the death of Joseph Larkin.

Maggie, about to refill the teapot, glanced over at Sam. He seemed exhausted. He was slumped forward, and his eyes were staring into space. The cup of tea Maggie had poured him an hour ago when he and Liv had arrived lay cold and untouched by his chair.

"Are you all right, Sam?" Maggie asked, cutting through the chatter.

"Can't imagine why he wouldn't be," Bert said. "It isn't like a man died in his restaurant five days ago."

"The police aren't giving you too much of a hard time about it, are they, Sam?" Helena asked. "I'm sure they won't shut you down—"

Sam gave a choked laugh. "I'm not particularly worried about being shut down at the moment," he said. "I think I've got bigger things to worry about."

The entirety of the MBC stiffened at the words, looking intently at Sam. Even Bert looked solemn.

"What happened?" Jim asked.

Sam heaved a sigh and rubbed the back of his neck. He looked as though he had aged a decade since Saturday. "I'm sure you know they're positive it was an allergic reaction?" he asked. Everyone nodded. "On Saturday, I told that detective that I didn't use peanuts or anything peanut-related in the restaurant. He asked if he could have some people take a look, and I said by all means. Turns out, there was peanut flour mixed in with the normal flour we use to batter the fish."

There was a long silence as everyone processed this new information. Maggie thought back to the strange, familiar taste of the fish. Now that she knew more, she could identify exactly what it had been: peanuts.

"You mean someone at the factory messed up?" Kate asked. "So they accidentally put flour in the wrong bag?"

Sam shrugged. "It's possible, but not very likely. We buy our flour in bulk and go through it fairly quickly. And peanut flour is expensive. I don't even think the brand we use makes peanut flour in the first place. It wouldn't make sense for it to be an accident. But I suppose we won't know until they test the rest of our flour to see if it's contaminated."

Maggie frowned. "Do you think someone deliberately added peanut flour and mixed it in so we wouldn't notice? Is that what you're saying?"

Helena gasped, her brown eyes wide as her hand went to her mouth. "They don't suspect murder, do they?" she asked.

"They haven't used those words exactly, and there's a chance we were just really unlucky, but it's suspicious enough that they want to ask me more questions."

"Why didn't you tell me?" Liv asked.

"I didn't want to worry you, love," Sam said. "And I only just found out about the flour today. I would have told you once I had got over the initial shock."

If there were a more unlikely couple than Sam and Liv, Maggie hadn't met them. Liv was meticulous, loved fashion and couldn't be seen in public with a broken nail or a strand of hair out of place. She was constantly on the lookout for new gossip and could read most people like a book. Sam, on the other hand, was laid back, didn't know Levi's from Ralph Lauren, and was content to keep to himself. But there had never been any doubt that they loved one another deeply.

Liv patted Sam's back reassuringly and he gave her a warm, but tired smile.

"If it is murder," Helena said, "it could have been anyone. I must say, it would be exciting, don't you think?" Helena was naively sweet and loveable, if a little eccentric. She was a reiki master and ran the local yoga studio and believed she had a psychic gift.

"No one's saying murder yet, Helena," Jim said. "But if it is, I'm pretty sure everyone in town would've had a motive. He wasn't exactly well-liked now, was he?"

"Of course he wasn't," June said.

"And everyone knew about his peanut allergy," Liv said. "Do you remember the time he had an allergic reaction at that cute little restaurant? This was years ago, of course. Right when he was starting to buy up all that property. He had an allergic reaction, then sued the owner for everything he had. Poor man lost the restaurant. A lot of people think it was fabricated or that Larkin ate the peanuts intentionally, but no one's been able to prove it."

"He's sued at least a dozen different places to get them shut down," Jim said. "I lost count of how many complaints he filed or how many people he tried to get me to arrest while I was on the force."

"I remember one time he hired me to fix his roof," Bert said. "Then refused to pay me."

"He was creepy, too," Kate said. "Remember when I worked as a lifeguard? He would always find excuses to come talk to me whenever I was in my swimming costume. I hated it."

They continued this train of conversation for the next several minutes, everyone theorising about who might have killed him—assuming it was murder, that is. There was still no concrete evidence. It could just have been an accident. But something about it didn't sit right with Maggie.

"Maggie, dear, these are delicious," Helena said after her third wagon wheel. She licked the chocolate off her fingers. "I don't know how you have the time to make them, but they are amazing. You really should think about selling them, you know. And I don't mean just handing them out here to customers in the shop."

June rolled her eyes. "I've been telling her that for years," she said. "But she goes temporarily deaf whenever I bring it up."

Heat rose up Maggie's face. "It's not something I've really considered," she said. "They aren't terrible, but I don't think they're good enough to sell or anything like that."

Helena snorted and shook her head. Her vibrant crimson hair swayed with the motion. "Really, you need to have more self-confidence," she said. "I think you should go talk to Abigail over at Seaside Sweets. If you won't listen to us, then you might just listen to her."

"I'll think about it." Maggie nibbled on a piece of shortbread, trying to figure out how to change the topic, and suddenly very self-conscious. But it turned out not to be an issue because the conversation quickly diverted back to the peculiar death of Joseph Larkin.

"Well, I suppose we'll know sooner or later," Helena said.

"Be honest, Sam," Bert said. "It was you, wasn't it? If you killed him, we won't turn you in."

June swatted Bert playfully on the shoulder, but Sam gave a small smile.

"You know you would be the first to know," Sam said.

"Yeah, I suppose you're right," Bert said. "Now, if it were me, I would have killed him at night and gotten you lot to help me hide the body."

"We know," nearly everyone said in unison.

~~~

As the meeting began winding down, Kate came up to Maggie.

"Let's walk home together," Kate said.

"Okay," Maggie said slowly. "That works for me. Let's go, Biscuit."

They waved goodbye to the rest of the group before stepping out into the night.

The combination of the pleasant summer breeze and the smell of the sea was always soothing, and Maggie took a deep breath as the two of them set off down the winding streets. At this time of night, their illumination consisted of street lamps, the moon, and lights streaming out of the pub and restaurants.

"So, what's up?" Maggie asked after they rounded a corner. "You haven't used the 'we need to talk' code phrase in a while."

Kate glanced up at the sky. In the darkness, her blonde hair seemed almost to glow. "This whole thing is weird," she said.

"You called a secret meeting to tell me that? I'm very aware it's weird," Maggie said.

Her cousin shook her head. "No, I mean it's really weird. There's no way this isn't murder. You have to know that, right?"

"I don't know anything."

"Of course you do," Kate said. "You're smart. You've read just as many mystery books as Mum. You can't just assume there's nothing strange here."

"Even if something strange is happening, that isn't something you needed to talk to me about in private," Maggie pointed out. "Everyone in the MBC agrees it's strange."

"I know," Kate said. Her eyes sparkled with intrigue and interest. "But that doesn't mean they're going to do anything about it."

Maggie rubbed her forehead and glanced over at her cousin. "I know that look," she said. "That's your 'I want to have an adventure' face." At 27, Maggie was four years Kate's senior. But that didn't stop Kate from roping her into some of her schemes.

"So?" Kate's eyes were the epitome of childhood innocence.

"Whenever you give me that look, we always end up doing something of questionable legality. I haven't forgotten the time you convinced me to sneak out of the house at 4 am because you wanted to watch the sunrise all the way over in Devon."

"You were twenty-one. You didn't sneak out."

"Then why did you have me climb out the window? Your mum shot me death glares for a week after she found out."

"What's the fun of an adventure if you don't venture into some grey areas of the law?"

"I can't believe I'm hearing this. Your dad's a former detective."

"Exactly." Kate held up a single finger, as if she were a teacher giving a lecture. "That means I always know how far is too far, and how much you can actually get away with."

"So, what is it you want to do, exactly?" Maggie asked.

"I want to investigate, of course," Kate said. She was practically bouncing with excitement. "A man died and was likely murdered in our friend's restaurant. We can't let that opportunity get away from us."

"We don't know he was murdered."

Kate rolled her eyes. "Yes," she said. "We do. And Sam is the main suspect right now. And if you say, 'we don't know that', I'm never dog sitting Biscuit again."

Maggie, who had been about to say just that, closed her mouth.

"The police will handle it," Maggie said. "If it was murder, he's innocent, and the police will figure that out soon enough. And what is it that you expect us to do? How are we supposed to investigate?"

"Well..." Kate drew out the word. "You told me that it looked as though there was a new constable, didn't you? And that he liked Biscuit—both the dog and the treat? We could always stop by and welcome him to Sandy Cove. I'm sure he'd appreciate it."

"You're impossible sometimes, you know that?" Maggie said, though not without some fondness. "There's no need to do any of that right now. If something happens—and that's a very big 'if'—I might reconsider."

Kate shrugged. "I give it a week," she said.

"What, a week until something happens?"

"Until something happens, or until your curiosity gets the better of you."

Maggie smiled and bumped playfully into Kate, who bumped back. Silently, they continued walking into the night, the conversation of Sam and the mysterious death behind them for the time being.

At least until something happened.

Chapter Five

"I THINK YOU WOULD like this one," Maggie told the teenage boy who was browsing the shelves. "It's perfect for a fantasy lover and should be a quick read."

The boy flipped through the book and silently skimmed the first page, his head cocked slightly as he considered it. He shut the book.

"Yeah, this looks fun," he said. "Thanks."

He picked up one of the biscuits that had been on the nearby table and bit into it as he read the back cover.

"You'll have to come back and let me know what you think of it," she said.

The boy nodded absentmindedly before turning and walking towards the checkout counter, where June was ringing up another customer. The shop was surprisingly full for a Monday afternoon, with people scanning the shelves or sitting in armchairs with cups of tea as they read the first chapters of books they were interested in. Some were even reading far beyond that, as though they weren't in a bookshop at all but in their own living rooms. Kate was also there as she was currently working in The Book Nook until she found a different job that interested her.

Everything seemed fine until Liv ran into the shop, the antique bell ringing with a greater sense of urgency than usual. Maggie had never seen her look remotely dishevelled before, but there was a first time for everything. Her shirt was crooked and her hair was all over the place. She was panting heavily and beads of sweat had gathered on her temples. It was clear she had run here as fast as she could.

"The police just brought Sam in for questioning," Liv exclaimed.

The slight hum throughout the shop vanished, eyes were torn from the books they were reading and now focused directly on Liv, some staring—including the teenage boy—with open mouths. Everyone waited with bated breath, eavesdropping eagerly. It wasn't surprising; everyone would know by now about Larkin's death at Sam's chippy. Maggie had been hearing gossip about it around town. But seeing everyone's hungry expression and desire to hear more put Maggie on edge. She considered making a distraction. Maybe knocking over some books or something else to give June and Liv some privacy.

June's eyes widened, then found Maggie. "Maggie, dear, would you take over the register for me?" Without waiting for an answer, June wrapped her arm around Liv and steered her into the office behind the counter, shutting the door behind them.

As Maggie rang up the till, firstly for a bemused-looking woman and then for the teenage boy, she strained her ears as she tried to listen in on the conversation happening beyond the door behind her. But that door was thick, and all Maggie could hear were muffled voices rather than any discernible words.

Kate, materialised by Maggie's shoulder, blue eyes wide and sparkling with interest.

"Did she say what I think she said?" Kate asked, staring at the closed door as if hoping to suddenly develop the ability to hear through walls.

"I think so." Maggie spoke from the corner of her mouth, even while she was smiling and handing a copy of *Beach Read* to the young woman on the opposite side of the counter.

"So I think that definitely qualifies as something happening," said Kate, not bothering to hide the eagerness in her voice. "Which means I was right. Even if I was a few days off the mark."

"Just because you were right doesn't mean we're going to do anything."

"Oh, come on," Kate said. "You can't tell me you aren't just as intrigued as I am…"

Maggie sighed and bit her lip while Kate stared on expectantly. The truth was, she was very intrigued. She desperately wanted to help Sam, and her own sense of adventure had been triggered. The only thing holding her back was the concern that they might get into some sort of trouble, but that was getting squashed by those other anticipatory emotions beginning to surface. Finally, after a moment, Maggie nodded. Kate silently pumped her fist.

The door to the office opened again, and the two girls fell silent as June and Liv walked out. Liv still looked slightly dishevelled, and now that her pulse had calmed a little, the ruddiness of her complexion had faded. If anything, she now looked a little too pale.

"I'm going to walk Liv home," June said. "I'll probably be gone the rest of the afternoon, if that's all right. You don't mind looking after the shop, do you?"

"Of course not," Maggie said, "take your time. I hope you start feeling better, Liv. I'm sure everything will turn out fine."

Liv nodded almost absentmindedly, and she and June walked out the front door. Maggie and Kate watched them until they vanished from sight. Then Kate rounded on Maggie. She didn't say anything, only looked intently at her cousin. It wasn't difficult for Maggie to spot the gleam of excitement in her eye.

Maggie knew that Sam being brought in for questioning changed the game. If the police ended up convinced of his guilt, then... it was not something she even wanted to think about. Neither Maggie nor Kate was the type to sit idly by, especially if they knew there was something they could do to help get Sam out of trouble. Maggie felt deep down that she would be able to find something that the police had missed. A piece of evidence, perhaps, or even just a clue. And if there was anything she could do to exonerate Sam, then they owed it to both him and Liv to take action.

"All right, all right," Maggie said. "We can go to the police station tomorrow."

Kate's eyes lit up with that trademark sense of adventure she always had.

"Can we go now?" she asked excitedly. Already she was reaching for Maggie's arm as if to drag her outside right then and there.

"Your mum literally just asked me to mind the shop," Maggie said. "So that's what I'm going to do." At Kate's crestfallen expression, Maggie sighed and said, "First thing tomorrow, I promise."

"Great!" Kate all but clapped her hands together. "Make sure to bring some of your biscuits."

"I don't remember Miss Marple bringing biscuits with her."

At the sound of her namesake, Maggie found Biscuit looking up at her, the dog's head cocked to one side excitedly. If she didn't know any better, she could swear that Biscuit was just as eager to crack the case.

~~~

The sky was overcast the next day as Maggie and Kate strolled down the hill from Maggie's parents' house. It had become Maggie's home, now that her parents had moved permanently to Spain after her father's retirement. The girls headed towards the centre of town where the police station was located. Maggie carried a small tin of biscuits in one hand while holding her Cavapoo's lead in the other.

Despite the slate grey of the sky overhead, it was warm, if not rather muggy. Maggie's shirt would be clinging to her back by the end of the day thanks to the humidity. But in the early morning, it wasn't too bad.

"Tell me about this new constable," Kate said.

"He seems nice enough," Maggie said. "The only thing I know is that he's very obviously new—he has that enthusiastic energy about him—and that he likes my dog and biscuits"

"Is he cute?"

Maggie laughed a little.

"A little too young for my taste," Maggie said. "But I suppose so."

It took about fifteen minutes for the three of them to reach the police station. Underpowered fans trying to combat the summer heat whirred and stirred the warm air as they stepped through the doors.

The station was small, but clean and obviously well-run. Diane, the middle-aged police officer looked up when the door opened, and she broke into a smile.

"Hello, Kate," Diane said. "How's your dad?"

"Enjoying retirement," Kate said. "He says 'hi,' by the way."

"Well that's sweet of him. And what about you, Maggie?"

"I'm doing okay," she said. "A little tired this morning."

"We were hoping we could talk to DI Pearce," Kate said.

"I don't think he's in yet." Diane stood from her chair and leaned over to look down the hall into the main area of the station, as though hoping she would catch a glimpse of him. "But I think Constable Brown is working over there. He's been helping Tom on the Larkin case."

Kate beamed, and Maggie knew that was what her cousin had been hoping for. "That will do just fine," she said.

Diane nodded. Then her face grew more sombre. "I heard about Sam," she said, her voice lowered to a conspiratorial whisper. "That's bad luck. He seems like such a nice man. It's hard to imagine him killing anyone."

"Don't worry," Kate said. "I'm sure that will clear up in no time."

With another cheery wave to Diane, the two walked past her and into the open space of the police station.

The clock tower beside the police station chimed half-past nine just as they reached Matthew's desk. He was hunched over, staring at the computer, and hadn't noticed Maggie and Kate approach.

Biscuit gave an excited, soft '*woof*' and walked around the desk to sniff at the constable's pockets. Matthew jumped, startled, as she pushed her nose against his trousers. He glanced down, and his eyes lit up, though this time it was tinged with a bit of confusion as well.

"Hello, girl," he said, rubbing her head. "What are you doing here?"

The young man glanced up. He first saw Maggie, then saw Kate. His jaw dropped open slightly for the briefest of moments but he quickly closed it again. Maggie wasn't surprised. Not only was Kate very pretty, but she also had one of those magnetic, vivacious personalities that seemed to enchant men.

"Hi!" Kate said, beaming. "I'm Kate. I think you've met my cousin, Maggie?"

"Cousin?" Matthew muttered, before looking over at Maggie. "Oh, yes, hi."

"Good to see you again," Maggie said.

"How can I help you. It's Miss Treloar, right?"

"You can just call me Maggie. I'd prefer it, actually."

"We just wanted to stop by and say hi," Kate said. "Maggie made some extra biscuits and thought you might like some."

"Biscuits?" His eyes trained on the tin. Maggie nodded and handed it over. He opened it and let out a low whistle. "These look amazing. Thank you."

"How do you like Sandy Cove?" Kate asked. "I can't imagine your first impressions have been particularly pleasant, considering a death was involved."

Matthew, who had just stuffed half a jam filled biscuit in his mouth, swallowed quickly in his haste to answer.

"Sorry," he said, "it's definitely not what I was expecting. These are delicious, by the way. They taste way better than the shop bought Jammie Dodgers I'm used to."

"Thanks," said Maggie, smiling. She tugged gently at Biscuit's lead as she tried desperately to get to the tin of biscuits.

"How long have you been here?" Kate asked, moving next to him and perching on the desk. "It can't have been long, otherwise, I would have met you by now."

Maggie stared at her cousin, trying to hide her astonishment. Was she... *flirting* with Matthew? Even if she wasn't, it seemed to be having an effect. Matthew's cheeks were turning a brilliant red, and he tried to avert his eyes from Kate

"Uh, I've been here for about a month," he said.

"How do you like it?" Kate asked. "It's a pretty small village. I can imagine someone who isn't used to it feeling a bit hemmed in."

Matthew laughed. "I'm actually from outside of Mousehole," he said. "It's even smaller than here. I rather like Sandy Cove, though."

"Even with the murder?" Kate asked, deftly steering the conversation back to the topic at hand. Maggie watched, unable not to be impressed. Kate knew exactly what she was doing.

"Well, that's certainly made it more interesting," he said. He had a biscuit in his hand and was twirling it idly as he looked up at Maggie.

"So, it was murder?" Kate's eyes widened.

Matthew was nodding. "It looks that way."

"Why do you think it was murder?" Maggie asked. Kate glanced over and gave her the biggest *I told you so* smirk Maggie had ever seen. She'd known Maggie would get invested sooner or later. Maggie resisted making a face back, too intent on hearing Matthew's answer.

"We interviewed all the staff," Matthew said. "And they all swore that they never used peanut flour in any of their food. But some of the men found an entire empty bag of it in the bins around the back."

"Were there any fingerprints on it?" Kate asked,

Matthew shook his head. "No, but the Detective Inspector thinks the owner might have something to do with it."

"Why would Sam have anything to do with it?" Maggie asked. "He's harmless."

"Well, not only does he have a motive—namely that Larkin had been trying to shut him down for years and even claims that it was Larkin who had posted all those negative reviews—but he's the main chef, and responsible for ordering and managing the food."

Maggie and Kate turned to look at a figure that had appeared in the doorway. DI Pearce was leaning against the door frame, arms folded. He clearly had been watching the trio for some time. His lips were shut tightly, but his eyes sparkled with amused exasperation. He pushed himself from the frame and strolled over.

"Perhaps our newest constable shouldn't be giving out confidential information to anyone who happens to walk in here."

"We were just offering him some biscuits," Kate said innocently. "Maggie made too many of them and it would be a shame for them to go to waste."

"In that case, he shouldn't be giving out confidential information in exchange for biscuits."

Matthew looked away sheepishly, a half-eaten Cornish fairing in one hand. Biscuit, seeing her opportunity, reached out and took the ginger biscuit from Matthew's grasp, chomping on it contentedly, her tail wagging.

DI Pearce leaned over and peered into the tin. With no change in expression, he plucked another fairing from the box. He took one bite, then paused, looking back down at the biscuit.

"I can see now how he was so easily taken in," he said, taking another bite. "You made these?"

Maggie nodded as heat rose to her cheeks under his stare.

Kate, seizing the opportunity to talk to a now-mollified Tom, asked, "Is Sam all right? We heard he was in for questioning."

"You don't need to worry about him at the moment," Pearce said. "He's not under arrest."

"But he's a suspect?" Maggie asked. "You know how mad that is, right?"

Tom gave Matthew a *how much did you tell them?* look, before turning back to Maggie. "As Matthew said, he had access to the food and a motive. And he had to have assumed Larkin would come at some point, if only to try and drive customers away. It was only a matter of time until he showed up."

"Sam wouldn't hurt a fly, though," Maggie said.

"Normally, I would agree with you," the inspector said, sympathetically, "but people can surprise you. And just because I like Sam and his restaurant, it doesn't mean I can write him off as a suspect. Especially when it comes to a murder."

"But—" Kate began, but fell silent when DI Pearce raised a hand.

"Right now," he said. "The best thing you can do to help your friend is to let me do my job. I know that isn't fun for you, but you will just have to trust me."

Kate looked as though she were going to object, but Maggie put a hand on her shoulder.

"I completely understand," Maggie said. "Thank you for your time, Detective Inspector. Please feel free to enjoy the rest of the biscuits."

"I'm certain they'll be put to good use."

Before Kate could protest, Maggie gently steered her cousin away from Matthew's desk, who looked a little sad to be seeing her go.

"Be seeing you," Maggie said, tugging at Biscuit's lead.

"Oh, and Miss Treloar?" DI Pearce asked, as Maggie and Kate made their way towards the door. "In the future, I'd appreciate it if you didn't use such an easy tactic to corrupt my constable into taking bribes."

His voice was stern, but the glint in his eyes belied his tone. Maggie had to prevent herself from smiling.

"Don't worry," Kate said, beaming. "We'll find something more subtle next time, I promise."

Chapter Six

"A MYSTERIOUS EMPTY BAG of peanut flour in the bin?" Helena asked, her eyes wide with fascination. "Then it must be murder."

"Seems a setup, if you ask me," Bert said, stretching out his legs. "Sam's smart enough not to dump evidence behind his restaurant. If it were him, he would've had it stashed in some unmarked container, just waiting for the perfect opportunity to use it. Then all he'd have to do is rinse it out, put normal flour into it, and Bob's your uncle, he gets away with murder."

"Anyone could have gone in and done the switch," Jim said. "He keeps the back door to the kitchen open so it doesn't get too hot in there."

"But we agree it's murder," Helena said. "I knew it. I just had one of those feelings—you know how I get those sometimes. Something was telling me it wasn't an accident."

"Yes, Helena, we all know it's murder now," said Bert. "You win the 'I Was Right' award."

The impromptu gathering of most of the MBC members happened organically from time to time when, as if all tapping into the same hive mind, everyone showed up at The Book Nook at the same time. It just so happened that the day after Maggie and Kate met with Matthew and Tom was one of those occasions. Everyone was gathered in one corner, lounging in the plush chairs and drinking tea, though June would periodically jump up from her chair to go help or ring up a purchase before returning.

"How are Sam and Liv holding up?" Maggie asked. Biscuit was resting comfortably at her feet, and she reached out to stroke the Cavapoo's soft, curly fur.

"About as well as you'd expect," Jim said. "I ran into Sam yesterday when we were surfing, but he wasn't in the mood to talk about it. Not that I can blame him."

"Oh, I wish they were here," Helena said. "At the very least, I'm sure that Maggie's baking would cheer them up." As if for emphasis, she took a bite of one of Maggie's homemade Jaffa Cakes, a recent baking experiment. Maggie had been perfecting her Jaffa Cakes for a few weeks. They consisted of a light sponge base topped with an orange-flavoured jelly that was coated in chocolate. There was always a debate about whether it was a biscuit or a cake. It seemed as though she had finally nailed the sponge texture, and for a change, the jelly hadn't turned rubbery.

"Ah, Liv would just complain that Maggie's sweets were going straight to her thighs," Bert said, but not without a hint of fondness. "Honestly, though, I don't know where you find the time to do all this."

"I've had a lot of sleepless nights," Maggie said, and Biscuit yawned on cue. "I don't think Biscuit's been particularly happy about it."

The dog looked up at her, giving her a look that, on a human, would have clearly indicated offence at the mistaken assumption. She let out a soft huff of indignation before laying her head back down on the ground.

"Have they found any other evidence?" Helena asked.

"If they did, DI Pearce stopped us before we could get it out of the constable," Kate said, her tone more than a little sulky. After they had left the police station yesterday, she had fully intended to go back later when the detective inspector might not be there on the pretext of retrieving Maggie's tin before Maggie had stopped her.

"Tom was just doing his job," Maggie said.

Her cousin rounded on her, one pale eyebrow perfectly arched. "*Tom*?" she asked playfully.

Maggie's cheeks instantly reddened. "It's his name, isn't it?"

Thankfully, June chose that time to refill everyone's teacup, breaking the conversation momentarily and preventing Kate from being able to respond properly.

"We should have asked what brand of peanut flour it was," Maggie said, changing the subject. "There can't be that many, and I'm sure it would have helped."

"It can't be cheap, either," Jim said. "I'd never even heard of peanut flour before."

"Me neither," Helena said. "What do you even use it for?"

"Presumably to make something taste more peanutty," Bert said, then dodged a swipe from Helena.

"But if it isn't Sam, who do you think it is?" June asked.

She had directed the question to her husband, but it was Maggie who answered.

"My guess is someone in the Larkin household," she said. "Or if it isn't them, someone who lives or works there knows something."

Everyone in the group was silent for a moment as they glanced over at Jim. He nodded his agreement.

"I agree," he said. "If one of the staff aren't involved, they at least know something."

"Do you think the police will figure it out?"

"Tom seems like the sharp sort," Jim said. "I don't think he'll stop at Sam. But I've been wrong about my fellow officers before."

"Whatever is happening," Maggie said, "we need to help Sam get out of this."

~~~

Maggie was pulling out a scalding hot tray of shortbread at the very moment her doorbell rang. It startled her and almost caused her to drop them everywhere. While hastily slamming the tray onto the worktop. She saved all but one, which was promptly and courteously removed by Biscuit in her effort to keep the kitchen immaculate. Once her heart rate went back to normal, she glanced at the clock. It was past nine. There was only one person who would ring her doorbell so late, and that was Kate. It was either her or a serial killer, Maggie wagered, a serial killer who didn't care for break-ins and instead politely waited at the front door.

Peeking out of the window, she saw it was the less sinister of the two and went to let her cousin in.

Kate was brimming with excitement when Maggie opened the door. Before Maggie could ask the younger woman what she was doing here, Kate brushed past her into the hallway.

"What's up?" Maggie asked. She didn't bother asking what Kate was doing here at this time of night: Kate was as much a vampire as she was when it came to sleeping habits, and it wasn't the first time Kate had dropped in for an impromptu late-night visit. Truth be told, she kind of liked them.

Kate's blue eyes shone excitedly, glinting with the 'I have a brilliant idea' look that always threatened trouble.

"You're not going to believe what I just found," she said.

"Let's hear it, then." It was obvious Kate was practically bursting to tell her.

Instead of speaking, Kate held out her phone. It was a job application site.

"Find a new position?" she asked.

"Just read it."

JOB: Housekeeper – 2 years experience required

"You hated being a housekeeper," Maggie said. "You quit after a month."

"The *whole* thing," said Kate, impatiently.

JOB: Housekeeper – 2 years experience required

Looking for a new housekeeper for a position in Sandy Cove. Must be attentive and meticulous. Will need to be able to remain on their feet for several hours and be willing to take orders without complaint. Must be used to potentially unpleasant tasks. References requested. £1,500/month with bonus for an exceptional job.

"Fifteen hundred a month?" Maggie's eyes all but bulged in disbelief. "You'd never be able to live off that. And who gets off on giving someone that little money and requests two years of experience?"

Kate rolled her eyes. "I don't care about the money," she said. "Look at the bottom."

Maggie obliged.

Inquiries should be directed to Amélie Larkin at alarkin@allardvineyards.com.

A. Larkin. Amélie Larkin. Now it made sense. Maggie looked up, dumbfounded at Kate.

"You can't be serious," she said.

But it was obvious that she was. It was evident by the determined and excited expression on her face. And what was more, Maggie could already tell that she had made up her mind. And she already knew what Kate was about to say.

"I've already applied," she responded, just as Maggie had predicted.

"A month's experience isn't exactly two years," Maggie said.

Kate shrugged. "It doesn't hurt to be a little liberal with the truth."

Maggie sighed. It was impossible to convince Kate to do anything else once she had made up her mind. "Just please don't ask me to lie for you," she said. "If I get a call from Amélie Larkin about your employment history as a housekeeper in my service, I'm going to tell her you were the worst housekeeper I've ever had."

"Technically, that's still lying," Kate said cheerfully. "Come on, Maggie. You're the one who said the family or staff probably had something to do with it. This is the perfect way for us to get in there to ask questions."

"Us?"

"Well, me, mostly, but naturally, you'd find excuses to pop in and check on your favourite cousin while she's working." When Maggie still didn't respond, she added, "Come on, you know you want to. It's a genius idea, if I do say so myself, and the perfect opportunity."

Rereading the job application over, Maggie couldn't deny that it was a good plan if they wanted to investigate. No one worth their salt was going to work for that little, especially if they had to relocate to

Sandy Cove. She wouldn't be surprised if Kate ended up being the only applicant.

Glancing up, she saw her cousin's eager face. She was going to do it no matter what, and doing it alone would be risky. She wasn't about to let her favourite cousin head into an unknown situation without help.

And on top of that, some part of her deep down yearned to investigate with her, regardless of what she said.

Taking a deep breath and running fingers through her auburn hair, she handed the phone back to Kate.

"All right," she said. "I'm in."

Kate squealed and hugged Maggie so tightly she could have broken bones.

"You're the best!" she said. "It would have been rubbish to do it alone.

Maggie smiled. Kate's personality was infectious. It was hard not to get excited along with her. She hugged her cousin back with almost as much enthusiasm.

"Just remember this the next time I ask you for a favour," Maggie said. "Actually, make that the next ten favours."

"Deal," replied Kate "Okay, let's go over the plan."

A loud crash from the kitchen stole their attention. Maggie rushed over. She ran in and stopped short when she saw the source of the commotion.

One of the trays of shortbread she had baked was overturned and on the ground. Still-warm biscuits had scattered everywhere, covering the tile floor in golden-coloured discs. And there among the wreckage was Biscuit, her tail wagging excitedly as if Christmas had come early. She chomped on one of the biscuits, swallowing it and promptly going for another.

"Biscuit, no," Maggie said. She tried to say it sternly, but she couldn't prevent the laughter from escaping. Biscuit had an addiction to all biscuits (except for chocolate ones, of course, which Maggie kept close guard on), but shortbread was by far her favourite. She reached out and grabbed the dog's collar, pulling her back away from the treats. "You're going to make yourself sick."

Biscuit cocked her head as she listened to Maggie, her tail still thumping as she looked up at her owner with adoring brown eyes. Then she tried to make a lunge for another biscuit, and Maggie promptly foiled the attempt.

"I told you that you shouldn't leave the trays too close to the edge," Kate said, bending down to pet the Cavapoo. "She's smart enough to pull them down if she can reach them, aren't you, girl?"

Biscuit licked her face.

Kate giggled and stood, wiping the dog slobber from her cheek. "I should probably get going. I just wanted to swing by and show you what I'd found. I'll let you know when I get the job," she said. She plucked one shortbread that had survived Biscuit's attempted heist from the baking tray and bit into it.

Maggie raised her eyebrows. "*When* you get the job? That's a pretty bold assumption."

"Oh, come on, Maggie," Kate said, strolling towards the door. She polished off the shortbread and licked her fingers. "You should know by now to never doubt me."

Chapter Seven

SURE ENOUGH, TWO DAYS later, Kate flounced into The Book Nook, a triumphant smile on her face.

"I've got a new job," Kate said.

"What?" June blinked, clearly taken aback. "What is it this time?"

The surprise wasn't unwarranted. Kate had never been particularly adept at keeping a job, though that was mostly due to her nature. She would find a job, work at it until she more or less mastered whatever it was, then leave when she got bored. To Maggie, she felt as though Kate would have been more at home in academia, where she could have spent the rest of her life learning. But that had never really interested Kate. She seemed far more interested in learning from real life than from a book.

"I'm going to be a housekeeper," she said.

"A housekeeper?" June's brow furrowed. "I thought you hated being a housekeeper."

"I decided to give it another go." Kate glanced over at Maggie and winked. It was a little too obvious, and even June noticed it. Her eyes narrowed.

"What scheme have you come up with this time?" she asked her daughter.

"What? Nothing!" Kate's expression was the epitome of innocence, but her mother didn't buy it for a second.

"Why do I feel like you're about to do something dangerous?" she asked. "Who are you working for?"

"Mum, stop worrying over nothing. How can a job as a housekeeper be dangerous?" Kate rolled her eyes, but Maggie noticed the way she had sidestepped the question about who Kate's employer would be. "Besides, I'm an adult."

"I thought you were going to look into culinary school," June said.

"I am, but culinary school is expensive. I can't exactly afford to go study at Le Cordon Bleu with what I have in my bank account right now, can I?"

June glanced over at Maggie, who was carefully trying to avoid eye contact with her, and was instead busying herself with reshelving a handful of books that people had placed on side tables and never returned after they had finished their tea and biscuits.

"Do you know anything about this?" June asked her.

"Who? Me?" Maggie was a lot less convincing than Kate, to the point where her cousin gave her an exasperated *are you kidding me* expression.

"What is it you two have planned?"

"June, it's nothing. Relax," Maggie said. "You don't need to worry about it."

"When Kate tells me I don't need to worry, I tend to worry," June said. "Do you know who it is?"

"No, of course not," Maggie said.

She would never be sure if June believed her, because at that point, the bell on the front door rang, and Bert strolled in. His eyes found Kate, and he immediately asked, "Kate, what's this I hear about you working for Amélie Larkin now?"

"What?" June's voice snapped.

"Thanks a lot, Bert," Kate muttered.

He held his hands up. "How was I supposed to know?" he asked. "Next time you want me to keep something from your mum, don't let me hear it from Tamsin Harris. She overheard that other housekeeper of Larkin's mentioning it earlier today and told me when I ran into her. I had no idea you were keeping it a secret."

June's eyes were closed and she was pinching the bridge of her nose. It took a moment before she opened them again.

"Kate," June said. "I love you, but this might be the worst idea you've ever had."

"Even worse than the time I dyed my hair pink?" Kate asked. "Look, relax. It's just a job. As a housekeeper. It's about as safe as possible."

"And this has nothing to do with trying to clear Sam's name?" June asked, her voice taking on a pointed tone.

"I need money," Kate said, her eyes once again wide with innocence. "If I happen to come across evidence that implicates someone else while I'm working for Joseph Larkin's widow, then I can hand the information over to the appropriate authorities."

"Kate, you're playing with fire." June shook her head and rubbed her temples. "You're a grown woman. I can't stop you from doing this, but please be careful."

"Don't worry, Mum," Kate said. "It'll be fine. I'm not doing anything dangerous. But I've really got to get going. I need to run errands before I start tomorrow."

Before her mother could say anything else, Kate had given her a quick peck on the cheek and darted out the door, waving behind her as she ran off.

There was a long silence after Kate left, none of the remaining three knowing exactly what to say. Then, June turned towards Maggie.

"You didn't have anything to do with this, did you, Maggie?"

Maggie didn't meet her aunt's stare. "No, of course not. But, uh, I just remembered I left something at home that I really need to go and get."

And she followed Kate's example and hurried out the door before June could interrogate her any further.

Or at least, she would have, had someone not opened the door at the same time as she was trying to leave, and had she not run straight into him.

The two stumbled as strong hands went instinctively to Maggie's waist in an effort to regain balance.

"I'm so sor—" Maggie cut herself off when she looked up and into the deep brown eyes of Detective Inspector Tom Pearce.

He looked just as surprised as her, but he smiled. This close she could see every one of his eyelashes. "No, no," he said. "I should have been paying more attention. You just appeared out of nowhere."

"Sorry about that," she said.

"Really, don't be. You're fine." He realised he was still holding her waist and released her.

"Did you come here for a book, inspector?" she asked, gesturing awkwardly.

"Tom, please. Inspector is a little too stuffy. And I was considering it," he said. "I love books, but I honestly never have the time to read. I'm trying to get back into the habit. Do you have anything you'd recommend?"

"It depends on what you like." Maggie brushed a strand of hair from her face.

"He strikes me as the mystery-lover type," Bert said.

Tom made a face. "They're fun on occasion," he said. "But they tend to hit a little close to home. I like fantasy for the escapism, and science fiction."

"For the spaceships?" she asked, a smile on her face.

"I was going to say I read them for dystopian allegories of socioeconomic problems, but really I just like the weird aliens and cool technology," he said.

Maggie smiled. "Have you read *The Three-Body Problem*?" she asked.

"A long time ago," he said. "But honestly, I'm in the mood for fantasy."

Maggie nodded in understanding. "Follow me, then," she said.

She led him through the shelves and into one of the corners of the library, where rows of colourful fantasy books lined the shelves, each spine presenting an esoteric, slightly ambiguous title for its novel. *Name of the Wind*, *The Priory of the Orange Tree*, *Neverwhere*, *A Wizard of Earthsea*. The wide array of names and how each one fit into their own story was always something she enjoyed.

Tom waited patiently as she ran her fingers across the spines of the books as she asked Tom questions about his interests. After only a handful of answers, she knew which one to pick. She tapped a title, pulled out the book, and handed it over to Tom. He glanced at it.

"*The Lies of Locke Lamora*?" he asked.

"It's Arséne Lupin in a fantasy Venice," she said. "More or less."

He raised his eyebrows and flipped through it. "Interesting," he said.

"If you're not convinced," she said, "you can sit in one of the chairs and read some. I can bring you some tea and biscuits if you want. Assuming you have time."

He raised his eyebrows. "Really?" he said. "Because tea and biscuits sound lovely. Matthew barely left me any of the ones you and your cousin bribed him with."

Maggie coughed sheepishly. "I don't know what you're talking about," she said. "But whenever you have the chance to bring back that tin, I'd really appreciate it."

"I'll make a note of it." He glanced around. "Any chair?"

She nodded, smiling. "Make yourself comfortable," she said. "How do you have your tea?"

"White and no sugar, thanks."

A few minutes later, Maggie returned with a cup of tea and a small plate of biscuits. Tom was relaxing in a plush red armchair, one ankle resting on his other knee as he continued to read. He was so engrossed in the book that he all but started when Maggie placed the plate on the table next to him.

"You like it?" she asked.

He nodded. "I'm not sure what I was expecting, but it certainly has a compelling start." He glanced down at the tea and biscuits waiting patiently for him. "I also wasn't sure you were serious about the tea and biscuits."

"It was Aunt June's idea when she opened The Book Nook," she said. "When she built it, she didn't want just another bookshop. She wanted a place where people could slow down and enjoy the books before buying, and she liked the idea of offering people food and drink if they wanted it."

"But doesn't that mean fewer people actually purchase the books?" he asked. "They might just stay here all day and finish it in one sitting."

Maggie laughed. "People do that at any bookshop," she said. "There was a time when I was in London that I ended up standing in the middle of an aisle for two hours by mistake and read an entire novella. I ended up buying it because I felt guilty. Anyway, people do that everywhere. I think it's more pleasant if they can at least enjoy themselves while they're doing it."

"Hmm. And you make all the biscuits?"

Maggie nodded. "Do you like them?"

"They're quite good, but I've never been one for Cornish Fairings, if I'm being honest."

Maggie raised her eyebrows. "Really? In that case, what do you like? I have others."

He grinned. "Now, where's the fun in telling you that?" he asked.

"That sounds like a challenge."

"Does it now?" He raised his eyebrows, his brown eyes dancing. "Then I suppose you best get baking."

Maggie pursed her lips, trying to hide her own amusement. "Are you sure this isn't just an attempt to get me to make you more biscuits?"

"Can't it be both?"

Tom grinned even wider and took a sip of tea, before looking at his watch. "I've got to get going. I was just taking a walk on my lunch break. Looks like I got a bit distracted." He stood and tucked the book beneath his arm. "I can pay for this up front?"

"See? Letting you relax and read in a comfortable chair convinced you to buy it."

"It helps that there's a talented saleswoman who knows how to pick books for indecisive detectives."

Maggie rang up his purchase, slipping the book in a bag and handing it over.

"Thank you, Maggie," he said. "Well, I best be off."

He took a step away from the counter, paused, then turned back. He plucked a ginger biscuit from the tray and bit into it.

"I thought you said you didn't like Cornish Fairings," Maggie said.

"Just because I don't typically like Fairings doesn't mean I don't enjoy eating quality ones." Tom grinned and waved as he stepped out of the shop. "Be seeing you. Thanks for the tea."

As soon as the door closed and Tom was out of sight, June and Bert, who had been lurking between the shelves unbeknownst to Maggie, emerged and gave her identical knowing stares of amusement.

"He was buying a book," she said defensively, not needing to ask what they were implying.

"Seemed like an awful lot of talking to buy a book," Bert said. "He seems like a nice guy, but I'd rather you not pick someone who might put my best mate in prison."

"It's not like that," Maggie said.

"We know," June said. "He's just giving you a hard time like always. We know you're not ready."

Maggie looked away, trying to find something to preoccupy herself with. Her eyes landed on Biscuit, who was resting on a chair, her eyes moving back and forth as she watched the proceedings even as her head never left the arm rest.

"I think Biscuit needs a walk," Maggie said.

The Cavapoo's head shot up at the word and with the energy and speed of a puppy, she hopped off the chair and darted towards the door, looking back over her shoulder to check that Maggie was following.

They stepped out into the brilliant sunshine and made their way down to the beach, in the distinctly opposite direction of Tom. The sights of the cosy shops on the winding streets were like a balm as she followed her normal path and reached the crystal blue ocean. The sun beamed down onto it, making the still water encircled by cliffs sparkle. The unceasing din of tourists and locals enjoying the weather and lounging on the sand reached her ears. She closed her eyes and took a deep breath, inhaling the sea air.

June hadn't been wrong when she had said Maggie wasn't ready for anything. Truth be told, she hadn't been ready for anything for nearly three years now. Back when she lived in London, she had met Simon and had fallen head over heels for him almost instantly. She still remembered how his skin had always been sun-kissed, despite the fact that he worked in an office—and forest green eyes. She remembered how he was tall and lean and blonde, with an easy-going smile that charmed everyone who saw it. She remembered the way he always made her feel special and wanted, the way his lips had felt against hers, and how his arms had wrapped around her. She remembered the way he had seemed nothing short of perfect for her.

She also remembered how, after a full three years of dating, she had come home from the library earlier than usual because she had developed a bad headache. It turned out that Simon had come home early as well, but not because of a migraine.

For a long moment after she saw him and the woman—someone from his work; Maggie never learned her name—she simply stood in the doorway, mouth open in silent astonishment. The image was almost too bizarre for her to believe it was true. But then Simon had seen her out of the corner of his eye and had pushed the woman away from him, though by then it was far too late.

She ran out before he could say anything.

That night, she slept over at a friend's flat after staying up past midnight eating ice cream and drinking wine with her. When she woke up the next morning, she had ten missed calls and twice as many texts, all from Simon.

It might not have hurt as much had they not been looking at rings the week before.

She moved out of their shared flat the same week, quit her job, and moved back to Sandy Cove. June had given her a position at The Book Nook immediately and she had tried to rebuild her life, and she'd met Biscuit not long after.

Now, sitting on the beach, watching as Biscuit bounded through the waves, barking excitedly, she had no regrets about leaving London, no regrets about breaking things off with Simon. But she did not want to let anyone in like she had Simon, and she probably wouldn't for a long time.

She pushed those thoughts from her mind. She had enough to worry about without dredging up memories of old flames. It was in the past now, and dwelling upon hurtful memories wasn't exactly the best way to move on. She had far more important things to think about.

Like the fact that Kate was determined to solve a murder. And that, at some point, Maggie had decided she wanted to, as well.

Chapter Eight

THE LARKIN MANOR WAS massive. When Maggie had first pulled up to the wrought iron gate, she had expected to be turned away. But when she explained she was bringing something to her cousin, the gate slid open with barely a sound, and she and Biscuit drove through.

The sprawling grounds were so green it looked almost artificial, the type of colour you might see in an animated movie instead of real life. Maggie drove by a tennis court that looked as though it had never been used and rows of flowers that she was positive weren't native to Britain. The lawn was immaculately kept, and the winding drive leading to the mansion was better kept than some of the streets in town. Off to one side, the ocean was visible over the edge of the cliff, sparkling like jewels in the sunshine.

And the grounds were nothing compared to the house itself.

The beautiful grey stone building towered over the circular drive. Each of the three stories was adorned with large windows that reflected the sun into Maggie's face. It was a prodigy house, with a symmetrical exterior, tower pavilions, and a perfect example of 18th Century architecture. The illusion of stepping into the Georgian period was only broken by the sight of an Aston Martin parked off to one side, currently being washed by a broad-shouldered, shirtless man.

She climbed out of her car, which suddenly seemed quite worthless and very much out of place, despite it being only one year old, and Biscuit followed. The man cleaning the car had stopped what he was doing and was watching her every move. He tossed the sponge into a sudsy bucket and came walking towards her.

"Can I help you?" he asked, smiling.

He was remarkably attractive, and it wasn't just because he was currently shirtless and muscular, his skin bronzed from the sun. His dirty blond hair fell lazily around his face, accentuating his high cheekbones and dashing smile. His jaw was chiselled, and it was hard not to stare.

Maggie hoped he hadn't noticed that she had frozen for a moment, a kind of malfunction from which she required restarting. She needn't have worried, however, because Biscuit had taken the opportunity to run over to him, her tail wagging exuberantly. The man kneeled down to pet her after letting her sniff his hand and getting the chuff of approval.

"Aren't you a pretty girl," he said, scratching Biscuit's sides. Maggie watched as the Cavapoo's foot began jiggling of its own accord. "What's her name?"

"Biscuit. I'm sorry for the intrusion. My cousin forgot her lunch," she said, holding up the lunchbox. "Her name's Kate, and she just started today."

The man's eyes went glassy for a moment before brightening with recognition. "That's right," he said, standing up. "I'd forgotten about the new girl. Right, let me take you around to the kitchen. "

"That's too kind."

"Not at all, I'm always happy to help."

The front door opened to reveal an austere-looking older man in a pristine black suit, presumably the man she had spoken to over the intercom at the gate. The shirtless man waved at him cheerily. "I've got it, Mr.Lawrence."

The man nodded, his eyes looking Maggie up and down with an impenetrable expression, before retreating back into the house and shutting the door.

"Mr Lawrence can be a bit intense. Figured you would rather have someone a bit friendlier show you around. My name's Peter, by the way."

"Maggie. Have you been working here long?"

"I've been working for the Larkins for a few years," he said. "I move between here and their London home with them."

"Do you like working for them?" With everything she knew about Joseph Larkin, it was hard to imagine that anyone could like working for them. But stranger things had happened.

"It's a job. Was never the biggest fan of Mr Larkin, but I don't think I was the only one. Though I guess it's just Mrs Larkin now. It's weird to think about. I'm mostly a handyman. It's not the most exciting thing, but it's a living, and you get some nice perks."

"Like driving that?" Maggie pointed to the Aston Martin as they walked past it.

Peter grinned that charming smile again. Just the look was enough to make a woman blush. "That's definitely one of the perks. I'm hoping I'll be able to get my own one day."

"The Larkins pay that well, do they?"

They followed a stone path that cut across the vibrant green grass as it passed rows and rows of fragrant roses, rhododendron, azaleas, and lavender. Everything screamed perfection and wealth in a way that made Maggie feel unnaturally small and inadequate. She gripped the lunchbox tighter.

Peter seemed to notice, because he gave a small chuckle. "I know what you mean," he said. "It's a lot to get used to. You should see their other home. It's even bigger."

"I didn't realise real estate paid quite this well," she said.

Peter gave a rich laugh that matched everything else about him. "No," he said. "Don't get me wrong, Mr Larkin made a good amount of money, but Amélie's on another level."

"Oh?"

"She owns Allard Vineyards in France," he said. "Well, Allard and a few others. And the wineries associated with them. She comes from old money."

That explained the 'allardvineyard.com' in the email address, at least. "Do you know if they kept their accounts separate?" she asked.

She doubted that a handyman would know that type of thing, but he surprised her. "She had him sign a prenup," he said. "And as far as I know, they had a joint account for household needs, and everything else was separate. The Allards—Mrs Larkin's family—have apparently all been notorious for wanting to make sure the money stays protected."

"That's a lot more information than I expected," Maggie said.

"When you're wandering around the house fixing things all day, you get to learn a few things," he said. "No one notices you."

Maybe Kate had the right idea after all.

They rounded the corner of the house, and Maggie was greeted by even more sprawling lawn. There was a great stone terrace behind the house, and steps that led down to a massive pool and adjoining hot tub down beneath. Oaks and chestnuts enshrouded the area, giving it a closed off and more private feel.

"Here we are." Peter pulled open a door, and a blast of cold air greeted them as they stepped inside.

Despite the exterior of the house looking like it could be used to film a period piece, the kitchen was incredibly modern. The stainless-steel appliances all glinted as though they were brand new. The gas stove was large enough to hold eight pots at once, and two ovens sat on top of one another, embedded in the stone wall. There was enough counter space, all dark granite, to lay out a spread for ten people.

Maggie's mouth dropped open. There were restaurants that didn't have as nice a kitchen. It was a baker's dream, too. The number of things she could make with this much space and half the equipment lining the wall...

She was still taking all this in when a tall man with russet-coloured hair came in from a door on the other side of the room. He paused when he saw them.

"Chris, this is the new girl's cousin." Peter's hand went to Maggie's shoulder. "Apparently, she forgot her lunch. Maggie, this is Chris, the Larkins' chef."

Chris looked young for a private chef. He couldn't have been much older than her. He nodded absently as he grabbed a large knife from a knife roll, the last name 'Tredinnick' embroidered on the front of the cloth, and began deftly slicing a tomato faster than she could blink. She took back everything she'd said about him not looking like a cook.

"She could have just asked me to make a little extra," he said, not glancing over. "You didn't need to come all the way out here."

He didn't say it in a brusque or rude way, or as if he'd been offended; he was simply stating the fact that it had been unnecessary and that he would have been happy to help. But he didn't look up from his work, now turning his attention to an onion.

"Or is it an allergy thing?" he asked. He glanced up, his face serious. "She didn't mention any, but people don't always think about it."

She couldn't have gotten a better opportunity if it had been delivered on a silver platter. "No, she doesn't have any," Maggie said. "But I'm not surprised your mind went there. I'm sure you're used to keeping an eye out for that sort of thing, considering Mr Larkin's allergies."

"It certainly made things a lot trickier," he said, and resumed chopping, this time thin slices of radishes. "But that's the way it goes sometimes. You get used to it. And nuts aren't difficult to keep out of the kitchen if you know what you're doing."

"It doesn't seem as though it took long for you to get them back here." Maggie pointed to the open pantry, where a jar of nuts lay in the middle of one of the shelves, perfectly visible for anyone to see."

"Mrs Larkin has a liking for them," he said, disinterested. "If you ask me, she wasn't torn up that much about her husband's death." He glanced over at Peter as he said that, who shrugged in a way that may have suggested agreement.

She certainly put on a good act the other day, then, Maggie thought, remembering how the widow had been in near hysterics during the whole ordeal. Something about the dichotomy between Amélie Larkin's reaction at Sam's restaurant and the fact that there were already peanuts in the pantry made her uneasy.

How much of the widow's performance the other day had been fabricated, and how much had been genuine?

Chris continued slicing the boiled eggs and throwing them into the bowl as he continued talking.

"Like I said, your cousin could have asked me to make more," he said, his head bent down. "Unless she doesn't like salad," he added, almost as an afterthought.

"I'm pretty sure Kate considers it a form of torture," Maggie said.

"She's just never had a good one, then." He was clearly engaged in the conversation, even though his focus never shifted from his work.

"And I never will," said Kate, emerging from the same door Chris had, and breezing through towards Maggie. It was bizarre seeing Kate in a uniform. She was wearing a black dress that landed mid-thigh and a white apron attached. Her blond hair was pulled back into a bun, and black stockings completed the ensemble. Maggie cocked her head, trying not to giggle at how her cousin looked in a housekeeper's uniform.

"Thanks so much, Maggie. I'm so sorry again, I know it must have been a headache for you to get all the way up here."

"A bit," Maggie said. "But it wasn't as though I was going to let you go hungry. Though I don't think I would have worried quite so much if I'd known there was a chef on hand."

Kate shrugged. "You know my relationship with salad," she said. "It's a hate-hate relationship."

"You really need to get better at eating your vegetables," Maggie said.

"But then I wouldn't have room for your biscuits." Kate had already opened the lunchbox and was digging through it until she came to the small bag. "Aha! Peter, Chris, you have to try these. They're delicious."

Without waiting to hear their confirmation, Kate had stuck a homemade Jammie Dodger into Peter's hand, and placed one of Maggie's Wagon Wheels on the counter next to where Chris was. Barely glancing over at it, and not stopping his preparations for lunch, the chef plucked it from the counter and ate it.

"It's good," he said. "Though next time, use a slightly darker chocolate. It'll help cut into the sweetness of the marshmallow. I've never been a fan of the jam variant, but it's a good balance besides that."

Maggie perked up instantly. She rarely had the chance to discuss the more technical aspects of baking with anyone.

"What per cent do you think?" she asked. "I used 60% this time, and I don't know how dark I can go without it being bitter."

"Around 70. That's what I use. Should create a good balance."

But before she could continue the conversation, Kate, who had already thrown the lunchbox into the fridge, grabbed Maggie's wrist.

"Come on," she said. "Let me show you the rest of the house. You'll love it. You too, Biscuit."

Biscuit gave a soft '*woof*' and trotted to catch up with them.

Chapter Nine

"YOU DON'T THINK THEY'RE going to get suspicious that you want to show your cousin the house?" she asked. "That's not something a housekeeper is normally allowed to do."

"Please," Kate said, rolling her eyes. "I've been here for all of four hours now, and I can already tell that Chris is way too engrossed in his cooking, and Peter is so absorbed in himself that neither of them is going to notice me showing my cousin around the house, let alone care. The only person that might make a fuss about it is Mr Lawrence, and I can plead the 'it's my first day' case if that becomes an issue."

Something prodded at Maggie's mind as she thought about Chris' last name. Tredinnick? How did she know that name?

The rest of the house was the complete opposite to the modern kitchen. It could have been out of a history textbook on Georgian architecture. The wide marble staircase sat at the end of the foyer, and the ceilings were stamped with beautiful and intricate designs. Carved wood made up several of the decorations, and the walls were simple but elegant panels. Even the furniture in the rooms they passed was styled to look as though it had come from that period.

"It's stunning in here," Maggie said.

"Really?" Kate asked.

"You don't think so?"

"Eh, it's not my thing."

They had just rounded a corner when they nearly ran into a woman in a uniform that was identical to Kate's. The girl started slightly, her large, hazel eyes growing wide.

"You scared me," the girl said, putting a hand to her chest. "You should make more noise next time."

"I'm so sorry," Kate said. "I'll be sure to be louder next time."

The girl nodded, tucking a short piece of light brown hair that had fallen from her bun behind her ear. She glanced over at Maggie in silent question.

"This is my cousin, Maggie," Kate said. "She brought me lunch, and asked if I could show her around a bit."

If there was any way to do it without the housekeeper seeing, Maggie would have stepped on Kate's foot.

"I'm Lizzie," the girl said, smiling. "I've been teaching Kate the ropes most of the morning."

"And I don't know what I would have done without your help," Kate said, beaming. "Seriously, do you mind if I keep showing her around?"

"Not at all," Lizzie said. "Just don't let Mr Lawrence or Mrs Larkin catch you. I'll be in the laundry room when you're finished. It was lovely meeting you, Maggie."

"You too." Maggie watched as the girl scurried away. Even though she had been friendly, she had seemed the nervous sort.

"She's sweet," Kate said, as if reading Maggie's mind. "I like her a lot. Let's keep going."

"So, what else have you learned in your four hours here?" Maggie asked as they roamed the house. She had no idea where Kate was taking her, so she just allowed her cousin to drag herself and Biscuit through the seemingly endless maze of corridors and rooms that made up the house.

"That Peter is a lady's man." Though Kate was ahead of her and Maggie couldn't see her face, she could hear the eye roll in her voice. "He started flirting with me in the first five minutes of my getting here. Did he do the same for you?"

"Possibly?" Maggie tried to think back on their conversation. "I wasn't paying much attention."

"You always were oblivious to that type of thing," Kate said good-naturedly. "But come on and keep your voice down, they just arrived."

"Who?" Though she obeyed Kate's request, she had no idea what she was going on about.

"You'll see."

They came to a door that was slightly ajar. Voices filtered through the opening, but it wasn't until they were right on the other side of the door that they became distinct enough for Maggie to identify with ease.

"Of course, I'm always happy to help the local constabulary with their investigations, but is it really necessary?" Mrs Larkin's voice conveyed the epitome of inconvenience, as if this were the greatest hassle she had ever had to endure.

"I'm afraid it is, Mrs Larkin." Maggie started slightly when she recognised the voice as that of Detective Pearce. "As I said, there's evidence that your husband was murdered."

"Yes, and I thought you already had a suspect," she said. "Why haven't you arrested him yet?"

"Because all the evidence we have is circumstantial, and we want to make sure we cover all our bases," Tom said.

Amélie gave a very audible and derisive sniff. "Well, if you don't arrest him, I plan on suing him, so at least there will be some justice, regardless of the police's competency."

"Mrs Larkin…" The forced politeness in Tom's voice was strained. "The day your husband died, you couldn't find his EpiPen in your purse. Do you normally carry it for him?"

"When we're out together, yes," she said. "He thinks they're too bulky."

"So, what happened that afternoon?" he asked. "Did you forget it? It wasn't in your bag."

"I most certainly did not forget it," she said. "I always double-check before we leave if I know we're going to eat out."

"So why wasn't it in your bag?"

"You're the inspector, isn't that your job to figure out?" Mrs Larkin's voice was testy and bitter, bordering on offended. "All I know is it wasn't there. Perhaps the business owner stole it while I wasn't looking."

"So Mr Murphy came near your table, then?" he asked.

"No, but he could have gotten one of his staff to do it for him."

"And you don't think you would have noticed someone rifling through your bag?'

There was a long silence at that. Maggie could picture Amélie Larkin, her fingers gripping the sides of her plush and expensive chair, her dark hair perfectly styled, and her make-up immaculate. She waited for the older woman's response, but it never came.

Instead, Tom asked, "Why were you out that afternoon, anyway?" he asked. "From what your butler told me, you have a personal chef who follows you wherever you and your husband go. Seems a shame to waste his talents and go eat at a chippy in town."

"It was his day off," she said. "And Joseph was craving fish and chips."

"Uh-huh, and are you sure it wasn't because Mr Larkin was attempting to shut down that establishment?"

Another long pause, this one far tenser than the one moments earlier. Maggie waited with bated breath to hear what the widow's response was.

"I don't know what you're talking about," she said. "And I don't appreciate the insinuations. My husband died just over a week ago. You should have some more respect."

"I'm just trying to get all the facts, Mrs Larkin," Tom said evenly. "I can't get to the bottom of this if I don't have all the facts."

"You have all the facts," Mrs Larkin snapped back. "Sam Murphy killed my husband because Joseph had the guts to complain about his subpar restaurant. It's not his fault if Mr Murphy can't keep a quality establishment."

"If it wasn't a quality establishment, then why did you and your husband eat there?" Tom asked. "I'm sure you could have afforded to eat anywhere in town. If you were so dissatisfied with Sam's fish and chips, then why go there at all?"

"Thank you very much for your questions, Detective Inspector, but I believe it's time for me to have lunch. I have a busy day ahead, dealing with my late husband's estate. I'm sure you understand." There was the sound of heels on tile, and Kate dragged Maggie down the hall a bit, opening a closet and pretending to be busy.

The door opened.

"I'll have Mr Lawrence see you out," Mrs Larkin said, her voice no longer muffled by the now-open door. Maggie peeked over. She couldn't see Mrs Larkin, and it didn't seem as though she was planning on exiting the room. Which meant Maggie would be able to avoid uncomfortable questions.

"No need," Tom said. "Thank you for your time, Mrs Larkin. We'll be in touch if we need anything else."

More footsteps, and Tom and Matthew stepped into the hall.

"I'm sure you will be," Amélie Larkin said, and slammed the door in their faces.

Tom and Matthew exchanged bemused glances, after which the inspector simply shrugged.

Before the two detectives could look in their direction, Kate and Maggie ducked back behind the closet door.

"Some people are just like that, Matthew," Tom said. "You learn to deal with them."

Maggie's skin crawled, and she let out a sigh of relief that they were at least hiding and had a chance of getting out of this unnoticed. However, there was a loud sound of something thumping on wood. Uneasily Maggie looked down to see her adorable Cavapoo looking up at her. Biscuit's tail was thumping against the door, very much visible to the rest of the hallway.

Footsteps grew louder, and a moment later, Tom appeared, his eyes landed directly on Maggie, and she realised that she wouldn't be able to avoid uncomfortable questions after all.

Chapter Ten

"MISS TRELOAR? MISS EDWARDS?" Tom asked.

"Hello," Maggie said, looking anywhere but at the two officers, too flustered to point out that she hated being called 'Miss Treloar.'

Biscuit woofed excitedly and bounded over to Matthew, eagerly licking the constable's fingers.

"Hey there, cutie," Matthew said, crouching down. Biscuit licked his face. "I'm sorry, I don't have anything for you today."

"I'm sure that if we'd known you were going to be here, we would have made sure to come better prepared." The implication in Tom's voice was clear as he eyed the two women. His jaw was clenched, but it seemed more like it was in order to maintain a stern façade than coming from a place of anger.

"Kate got a job," Maggie said, nudging her cousin. "I only came by to bring her lunch."

She was dying of embarrassment. She should have known all of this was too easy. The fact that DI Pearce just happened to have come to the manor today of all days was some of the worst luck imaginable. She knew he could see right through her lies,

"Ah." Tom nodded thoughtfully. "I'd forgotten people like to eat in corridors. Without food."

"I had to put up linens," Kate said innocently, putting up the stack of white folded sheets that she had just pulled out moments earlier. "Work before food; you know how it is."

"How convenient."

Biscuit, who had seemingly decided she had greeted Matthew enough, went over to Tom now, her tail wagging as she sniffed at his trouser leg. Tom smiled and bent to scratch her ears.

"Tell me," he said. "Do you bring the dog with you everywhere in order to distract and placate officers of the law, or because you simply like her company?"

"The latter, obviously. Though she helps with the former as well." Maggie scrambled for something innocuous to say, trying to change the subject as that feeling of scrutiny continued to overwhelm her. "How have you been enjoying the book?"

"Unfortunately, I think I was overambitious when I purchased it," he said. "I've been too busy to pick it up again."

"Does that mean you don't think Sam is guilty anymore?" she asked, hope rising in her chest.

The smile playing on Tom's lips faltered, and that told her everything she needed to know. Her own cheerful demeanour slipped away as the full implication of the expression registered.

DI Pearce must have noticed the shift, because he raised his hands in an almost defensive gesture.

"I'm not saying anything one way or the other," he said. "I don't know if he's guilty. But I have to check every option regardless of my personal feelings."

Kate, however, was far less diplomatic. She crossed her arms and shot daggers at Tom, who looked away. Biscuit looked up at Kate, then over to Tom, her tail wagging slowly and uncertainly, before huffing and trotting over to stand next to Kate.

"See?" Kate said, scratching Biscuit between the ears. "Even Biscuit agrees with me."

"And as much as I would love to have a character witness from such an adorable dog, I don't think it would stand up in court," Tom said. "They tend to be most effective when they're actually able to speak."

"That just goes to show you how broken the judicial system is nowadays," Kate said, sniffing derisively, and it sounded so genuine that Maggie had to wonder if she legitimately meant it or was joking.

"If it makes you feel any better, we do have other suspects," Matthew said hurriedly. "That's why we're interviewing the staff. And then there are Mr Larkin's business partners."

Maggie straightened, her eyes flashing over to Tom, who now looked mildly irritated.

"Yes," he said, glancing meaningfully over at his constable, "though normally that's not something we divulge to whoever asks."

Matthew sheepishly looked away.

"Anyway," Tom said, looking back at Maggie, "I can't really talk about it. Yes, Sam is still under suspicion. But we haven't taken him into custody yet, which I'm sure you know. Besides that, I can't tell you much. Regardless of how many biscuits you attempt to bribe me with."

"We were just being hospitable," Maggie said innocently. "And I can't help it if Biscuit is now obsessed with Matthew."

She looked pointedly over at the Cavapoo, who had already abandoned her post next to Kate in favour of going to Matthew, looking up at him and wagging her tail.

"I told you not to give her biscuits," Maggie said.

"Honestly, I don't know how you can say no to her at all." Matthew scratched the dog under the chin, and she panted happily. "She's so sweet. If you ever need a dog-sitter..."

Tom cleared his throat. "Before you finalise the terms of your side job, we might want to finish interviewing the staff."

"Right. Sorry, sir." Matthew stood up. He gave a friendly wave to Maggie and Kate before following the inspector down the corridor.

"Well, that was fun," Kate said once they were out of earshot. "Do you think we can listen in to their other interviews?"

"I think we've run out of potential excuses," Maggie said. "And I'd rather not get on Tom's bad side." That, coupled with the entire conversation, had only intensified the sense of being an interloper that had been creeping up on her the entire time she'd been here.

"Wouldn't you now?" Kate gave Maggie a knowing look. I wonder why."

Maggie ignored her, instead attempting to change the subject. "Why don't we eat?" she asked. "I'm starving, and I packed enough in that lunchbox for both of us."

"How convenient of you," Kate said. "One would almost think that you wanted to stick around for a bit longer."

"You're not the only one who wants to solve this mystery," Maggie said, giving her cousin a playful nudge.

"I knew I'd be able to get you interested."

"Don't flatter yourself. I was always interested. You just made it a lot easier for me to get involved. Now come on, I made pasties."

"Why didn't you say so earlier?"

A few minutes later, Maggie and Kate were in a small room that had been set aside as a break area for staff. It was a nice space with plenty of sunlight streaming in through the windows, an espresso machine, and a half-full 'snack fund' jar to help stock the communal snacks tucked away in one of the cabinets. People's belongings were tucked away in locked cubbies, and the entire set-up had a pleasant, cosy feel, which surprised Maggie somewhat, given her knowledge of the Larkins lack of generosity.

"Clearly they suspect Mrs Larkin of doing something," Kate said after swallowing a bite of pasty. She spoke in a low voice as if worried someone could hear them in the otherwise empty room. It made Maggie wonder if there were microphones, and her stomach churned as her brain reminded her she was effectively an intruder here. "I can't blame him. She was supposed to carry around his EpiPen. It seems strange that something that important would go missing without her realising it."

"Stranger things have happened," Maggie said. "And it seems too obvious. I mean, her not having the EpiPen is a glaring red flag to me. Mrs Larkin is smart enough to think of something far cleverer than that. Besides, if you ask me, if Mrs Larkin were a murderer, she would be just the kind to use poison."

"You barely know her!" Kate said, both a little shocked and thrilled by Maggie's assessment.

"And you've known her for a handful of hours," Maggie said. "That's not much better."

"All I'm saying is I wouldn't be surprised if she was guilty."

"Hmm…" Maggie drummed her fingers on the table as she watched the steam rising from the re-heated pasty in front of her. The delightful scent of potatoes, beef, and seasoning wafted up towards her. Down at her feet, Biscuit was whining softly, trying to find a way to get to the table and devour the pasty without her owner noticing. "What motive would she have? It can't be money. From what I've heard, she was richer than Larkin himself."

"Maybe she just hated him and wanted out," Kate said. "Or any number of reasons. I just don't think she should be ruled ou—"

She cut herself off as the door opened. Lizzie walked in, her face a little pale. Maggie jumped, face heating as she scrambled, trying to to figure out some way of explaining her presence. But Lizzie didn't seem to care. She gave a shaky smile when she saw the other two.

"Has the detective talked to you yet?" she asked, walking over to sit down at one of the empty chairs. Her leg jiggled up and down, creating a light rhythm against the floor.

"We ran into him," Kate replied carefully. "But that's about it. I don't think he considers me remotely interesting, considering I started after Mr Larkin died."

"Lucky you." Lizzie realised she was biting her nails, and quickly crossed her arms.

"I'm sure you have nothing to worry about," Kate reassured. "He's just covering all bases. If he thinks you had anything to do with it, then he's dumber than a sack of rocks."

Lizzie's lips pursed in what was almost a smile. "You may be right," she said. "It's just nerve-wracking, you know? He was asking me what I was doing that day and what the Larkins were like as employers."

"What did you tell them?" Maggie asked.

"The truth." The housekeeper hesitated as if she was considering adding something. Something in her eyes told Maggie she had decided against whatever she was about to mention, and instead Lizzie said, "I was in town that day. It was my day off and I happened to be lounging on the beach."

"Ah," Kate said.

"What did you say about the Larkins?" Maggie asked.

Again, she hesitated. "I told them that they were good employers," she said. "Though I wished that they paid me a bit more."

Maggie didn't press the matter, but she did take the opportunity to study Lizzie, and concluded she was younger than Kate. She had a sweet, heart-shaped face that complimented her large hazel eyes. A little pinched, perhaps, suggesting she didn't eat quite enough. But there was something brimming under the surface, some sort of unspoken anxiety that she wasn't going to share. She thought about pushing the matter, trying to see if she could get any more information out of her, but she thought it best to bite her tongue. She was already clearly nervous, and Maggie didn't know her well enough to pry information out of her subtly. But the more she glanced over at the woman, the more she was certain that there was more going on than met the eye.

The door opened again, and the tall, austere man in the black suit stood in the doorway. His thin lips were a straight pencil line, and there were deep wrinkles along his mouth and brow. His posture was perfect, and he looked at Maggie with an almost imperial stare that radiated authority, and, potentially, a sense of superiority.

Lizzie started, eyes wide with something akin to fright. Just the look in the housekeeper's eyes was enough to make Maggie's own heart begin pumping faster with unease. Lizzie stood and excused herself, hurrying out one of the side doors and carefully avoiding the newcomer.

"Good afternoon," the man said. His voice was slightly husky, but stilted and formal. "I do not believe we have met formally."

"This is my cousin, Maggie, Mr Lawrence," Kate said, continuing to sit. "She came to bring me lunch."

"Ah," Mr Lawrence said. His eyes didn't leave Maggie, and she suddenly felt like a rather uninteresting ant being studied beneath a microscope. "Normally I do not allow staff to socialise on the job, Miss Edwards." Then his eyes went to Biscuit and his eyes narrowed. "Nor do I allow dogs on the premises."

"My apologies," Kate said. It was clear she was biting back the retort she wanted to give, doing her best to look chagrined, her face slightly downcast and looking towards the man's feet instead of his face. From Maggie's perspective, it seemed as though she was doing her best to be nonconfrontational to keep her job. Maggie, on the other hand, felt her face prickle with embarrassment and unease at the steward's glower. "I didn't realise."

His gaze was unwavering, his expression inscrutable. Maggie suddenly wanted to find a nice big rock to hide under.

"I would appreciate it if neither you nor your dog came back in the future," Mr Lawrence said to Maggie directly, before addressing Kate. "I would suggest you get back to work as quickly as possible."

Without even waiting for their response, he left the staff room and shut the door behind him.

"Charmer, right?"

"He's certainly something," Maggie said, her eyes still locked on the door as unease rippled through her body in nauseating pulses. "I can't believe the 'it's my first day' excuse actually worked."

Her cousin gave a mischievous smile and said, "Told you it would."

"I should get going," Maggie said, getting up. "I don't want to get you in trouble and, regardless of your motives for being here, you still have a job to do."

"I know," she said, deflating a little. "At least I'm getting paid for it."

"That tends to be the definition of a job," Maggie replied, eyes sparkling. She giggled as Kate bopped her lightly on the head.

As Maggie stepped out into the bright sun, that oppressive unease seemed to lift, and she took a deep breath of fresh air before her attention was drawn towards the pool. She found Amélie Larkin stretched across a lounger, modelling a flattering black bikini and lightly holding the stem of a champagne glass between her fingers. Not too far from her stood Peter, still shirtless, holding a pool skimmer and leaning on it like it was a walking stick. His mouth was moving, but she was too far away to hear anything that he was saying. After a moment, Peter dipped the net into the water and drifted it across its surface.

~~~

The kitchen was filled with the delightful scent of baking biscuits as Maggie wiped down the counter, getting rid of the flour and sugar that had inevitably escaped during the biscuit-making process.

"I'm not sure how much we learned, to be honest," Maggie said as she continued to clean. "Nothing ground-breaking, except that I need to use darker chocolate in my wagon wheels. But I guess it's only been one day, so how much are we really going to find out in that time?"

The timer dinged, and Maggie hurried to the oven, opened it, rotated the baking sheet, and closed it again.

"I mean, we know that it was the staff's day off," she said, punching buttons on the oven and resetting the timer. "And we know that Amélie always carried around her husband's EpiPen. We know Tom and Matthew have at least considered the possibility that Amélie or a member of the household could have done it. But besides that, I'm not sure. What do you think?"

Maggie looked down at Biscuit, who was sitting just inside the kitchen. Her head was tilted to one side as though she were listening intently. It was an old habit of Maggie's to talk to Biscuit as though the Cavapoo actually understood what she was saying. It helped her parse out her own thoughts and to sort out what was going on and what to do next.

"I know," she said, brushing a bit of flour off her shirt. "I need to find a motive. We don't even know why he was killed. It could have been a myriad of things: greed, revenge, or perhaps someone just wanted him silenced. If we can figure that out, it'll help narrow down the suspects. And Kate's probably in the best position of anyone to gather other clues."

Biscuit woofed as if in agreement. But Maggie knew better.

"The shortbread isn't ready yet," she said. "You'll have to wait."

Biscuit woofed again, disappointedly, and lay down, her eyes never straying from the oven.

Chapter Eleven

THE SKY WAS OVERCAST and the air was muggy the following day as Maggie stepped out of the house with her Cavapoo. She had a tin of biscuits in one hand and Biscuit's lead in the other. An umbrella dangled from her wrist as she glanced up at the sky, half expecting to feel raindrops dotting her face. But the steel grey clouds didn't seem ready to release their deluge, so she set off down the sloping street.

From this vantage point, slightly above the lower parts of town, Maggie was able to see right across Sandy Cove. The panoramic vista that stretched before her, revealed the coastal village in all its picturesque glory. The houses and shops below seemed dipped in a palette of confectionery colours, reminiscent of lollies arranged in a sweetshop window. They ranged from soft pastels to vibrant, sun-kissed hues, creating a mosaic of eye-catching charm. Amidst this kaleidoscope, the church's spire soared toward the heavens, a steadfast sentinel that pierced the sky above the candy-striped buildings. As the brisk wind tugged at her auburn hair, seagulls cawed far off in the distance. As she stood there enveloped in the colours and sounds of Sandy Cove, Maggie felt as though she had stepped into a living watercolour painting where every brushstroke blended harmoniously into a scene of unrivalled beauty.'

It was strangely quiet for mid-morning, even by Sandy Cove standards. But that didn't bother Maggie. She wandered lazily down the road, letting Biscuit stop to sniff the flowers or do her business. They weren't in a hurry; the only possible deadline was that of potential rain, and it felt nice to take her time, something she never felt like she got to do anymore.

Eventually they arrived at Seaview Street, which was blocked to traffic. There were lots of interesting shops, cafes and restaurants along the cobblestoned street that lined the beach and harbour, including Sam's. On sunny days the road was packed with people visiting the shops and restaurants, stopping to look at the train in the toy shop or to watch Abigail or one of her staff decorating biscuits in the window. Children would be carrying cones from the ice cream shop, the ice cream already melting as they charged down the street.

The rain seemed to have frightened off most of the tourists and the sound of laughter and delighted screams that normally filled the air were softer and far more subdued. But the dimness from the cloud cover did not take away from the charm of the area.

Sweet Treats was empty when Maggie pushed the door open. Abigail, a petite blonde woman with a perky face and brilliant green eyes, looked up from where she was scribbling in a ledger. Her eyes lit up and she beamed.

"Hi Maggie," she said. "And hello to you too, Biscuit."

Biscuit wagged her tail, barely noticing Abigail as she sniffed excitedly at the display case filled with a delightful array of freshly baked biscuits. The selection included shortbread, Cornish Fairings, Empire biscuits, Millionaire's shortbread, Viennese Whirls, macarons, and iced biscuits decorated as mermaids, seashells, and pirates. And that was just the biscuit case. Another showcased tempting cupcakes, cakes and tarts. Yet another displayed Abigail's more technical and delicate pastries, mousses, and cakes. The entire shop enveloped Maggie in the mouth-watering aroma of sugary delights, sparking a longing for a sweet treat for herself.

"Sorry," Maggie said, trying to tug Biscuit away from the display case. "Biscuit, say hello to Abigail."

Biscuit, suddenly remembering her manners, abandoned her ogling of the display and ran over to Abigail.

"What can I do for you, Maggie?" Abigail asked, holding out some shortbread for Biscuit.

"Helena's been pestering me for weeks to come talk to you," she said. "She wants me to show you some biscuits."

Abigail smiled, "She told me last week I should expect you," she said. "And that I should come find you if you didn't show up."

Maggie's face turned a brilliant pink and her cheeks burned. "I should have guessed she'd try something like that," she said.

"That's Helena for you. Are you really that surprised?" Abigail asked, laughing a little. She leaned closer against the counter, eyeing the container that Maggie was clutching in her hands. "Show me what you've got," she said.

Feeling suddenly even more self-conscious, she placed the biscuit tin next to the register and carefully opened it, revealing an array of delights inside.

"Homemade Wagon Wheels and Jaffa Cakes," Maggie said. "I'm pretty sure these are two you don't offer."

"I've always wanted to," she said, "but I don't have the time to make them."

"Also, I just brought some of my shortbread. At least Biscuit's a big fan. Though I'm really not sure about my Jaffa Cakes. I think there must be something off with the recipe. I've never been entirely happy with them." Maggie was already regretting bringing anything in at all and suddenly realised that even just a nibble from someone of Abigail's expertise would expose her creations as amateurish imitations. "I thought maybe you could help me figure out where I'm going wrong."

Abigail was scanning the contents with the studious air of an art scholar examining miniature *objets d'art*. She plucked a Jaffa Cake from the tin and bit into it. She chewed for a moment and Maggie watched her as she carefully tasted it, knowing full well that she was scrutinising every flaw that could be found within that little bite, from the flavour to the texture and back again.

"Do you make the jelly yourself?" she asked. Maggie nodded. "You might want to add a touch more gelatine. It still holds up nicely as it is, but half a sheet more would help it stay firm on a hot day while the chocolate is trying to melt. Do you use orange zest or just the juice?"

"Both," Maggie said. Abigail nodded her approval, then popped the rest of the biscuit in her mouth.

"Might want to add a bit more zest. Good sponge, though," she said, more so to herself than to Maggie. Next, she plucked out a Wagon Wheel, examining it with the same amount of care and diligence that she had shown the Jaffa Cake. When she bit into it, she could not help but close her eyes in what looked to Maggie like a little moment of ecstasy.

"Now these," she said, holding up the half-eaten Wagon Wheel. "Are perfect. Absolutely no notes."

Thank you, Chris, Maggie thought.

"Really, Maggie, you are way too hard on yourself. These are good. Really good. In fact..." Abigail said, peering into her biscuit display cabinet and pushing one tray along, "I've got some space right here. Would you be willing to bake them for me? I've been wanting them in my shop for ages. My customers would love them."

Maggie blinked as the words set in. Then she burst into a grin.

"That would be fantastic," she said, too stunned to even laugh. "Thank you!"

Abigail's smile faltered. "There is one catch," she said. "I can't really pay you that much at the moment."

Maggie tilted her head, frowning. "Is the shop not doing well?" she asked.

"It's doing okay," Abigail said, a little unconvincingly. "But the rent keeps skyrocketing. You know how it is right now."

Maggie nodded sympathetically. "You know what?" she said. "You don't even have to pay me at all. I'm just flattered you liked them enough to even offer."

"Nonsense! Of course you're going to get paid. How about I pay for any baking ingredients you use exclusively for these two, and 50% of whatever they bring in?"

Maggie blinked and instinctively glanced down at Biscuit as if to confirm they had both heard Abigail correctly. The Cavapoo looked up at her, her tail wagging hopefully, adorably oblivious to everything that was going on between the two humans, her only interest currently in the delightful biscuits just out of her reach.

"Um," she said, looking back at Abigail. "Considering I was just coming in here to ask you what was wrong with my Jaffa Cakes, that seems incredibly generous."

"I can take that as a yes, then?"

"Absolutely," Maggie said, nodding fervently even as she was dealing with the initial shock. Abigail liked her biscuits enough to pay her for them. The thought was so absurd that she almost thought she was dreaming. But something else filtered into her thoughts as the shock began to subside a bit. "You really don't have to, though, especially if the business isn't doing well."

Abigail rolled her eyes. "I'm fairly certain we went over this about two minutes ago. Of course I'm going to give you something for your trouble. And I'm excited to sell these biscuits." She paused and lowered her voice a little. "Though in all honesty, I don't know how long I'll be able to."

"How come?"

"I'm considering selling," Abigail admitted. "To get out while I can still make some sort of profit. I haven't decided anything yet, but it's been on my mind for a while, and I started considering it more seriously when someone approached me out of the blue with an offer the other day."

"Wait, who?" Maggie asked, a little worried.

Abigail seemed to read her mind because she laughed. "No," she said. "Joseph Larkin didn't rise from the dead and lurch into here looking for one final business deal. It was George Evans, who is very much alive."

"Really?" That was news to Maggie. George Evans was another very wealthy businessman, though far more tolerable than Larkin had ever been. He lived in town full-time and had always seemed the type to invest back into the community. It wasn't shocking that he was trying to buy property, especially on the coveted beachside stretch of little shops, but the timing of it felt incredibly fortuitous for Evans.

"What about Larkin?" she asked. "Did he ever give you an offer?"

Abigail snorted derisively. "Of course. He offered to buy it for less than what I purchased it for eight years ago. George gave me a much more reasonable offer."

"Do you know what he wants to do with the space?" Maggie asked.

"No idea," Abigail said. "I actually asked him that very question, and he gave a weird, vague answer about restructuring the area. It's the main reason I'm hesitating at the moment. That, and I'm waiting to see if I'm just experiencing a natural dip in business that may correct itself sometime soon. It happens from time to time. I'd rather not sell, but if I do, I could just downsize to a smaller shop somewhere away from the beach. But I'd miss Seaview Street, and I always liked decorating biscuits in the window for the passing tourists. Anyway, there are no promises yet, but we'll see."

"I hope you stay in business," Maggie said. "And that's not just because it's now a side gig for me."

Abigail laughed. "How many do you think you can make in a week?" she asked. "Realistically, considering your schedule and how long they take?"

Maggie did some calculations in her head and considered how much free time she currently had, given everything that had happened. "Thirty of each? Thereabouts?" It would involve baking most nights, but it would be worth it. Any excuse to bake was enough for Maggie to reach for her apron, but the thought of getting paid, something she'd always dreamt about but never thought would actually happen, was an even greater motivation.

Abigail nodded. "Seems reasonable," she said. "If you end up having time to make more, that's great. Bring them in whenever you can so that they can be fresh. Do you want me to have someone draw up a contract?"

Maggie laughed. "I don't think that's necessary," she said. "I trust you. But if you want one, we can talk about it."

"Let's see how this goes and we can finalise the details later."

Maggie smiled and nodded. Biscuit began to whine and looked at Maggie with pleading eyes. "I've got to get going," she said. "But before I do, I think I have to buy Biscuit something before she goes mad."

As if on cue, Biscuit began to do her 'excited dance' where she pranced elatedly and gave soft but enthusiastic barks.

Abigail grinned and plucked out a dog-friendly peanut butter and banana biscuit from a glass jar on the counter and tossed it to Biscuit, who caught it in her mouth and began chewing eagerly.

"It's on the house," she said, and waved as Maggie and Biscuit walked out the door.

~~~

"George Evans... Really?" Bert asked as the MBC congregated at the Smuggler's Inn, a traditional English pub adorned with plenty of hardwood, plush booths, and golden lighting. The bar, a beautiful mahogany piece, boasted shelves filled with various bottles of booze, their numbers seemingly doubled by the reflection in the mirror behind. The room buzzed with the lively din of predominantly local patrons, filtering in for dinner and eager to catch the end of happy hour. Though not yet packed, in a couple of hours, it would become standing room only at the bar with a thirty-minute wait for a table. Every time the kitchen door swung open, tantalising scents of frying food and grilling burgers wafted through the air, enough to make Maggie start to salivate.

The MBC had taken over two of the booths beside the bar. Bert was on his second beer of the evening, Jim and Sam on their first. Kate and Maggie were both nursing glasses of wine, while Liv, June, and Helena were each drinking cider. It was a lively evening, livelier than their last couple of get-togethers had been. Sam seemed less pallid, as did Liv, and their lifted spirits did wonders for everyone else.

At first, the group had been hesitant to even mention the case, stepping delicately around it to avoid upsetting Liv and Sam. But that stopped when Liv said, quite matter-of-factly, "Stop treating us like China dolls. We know you want to talk about it and we want this case solved more than any of you. So what are your theories?" At which point, after a slightly stunned silence, Maggie had timidly brought up George Evans.

"He always seemed like the decent sort," Bert said, "though if he's trying to buy up property the week after his competitor died, that seems pretty suspicious, don't you think?"

"People are weird," Jim said. "My bet is he's just seizing the opportunity."

"I don't know," Helena said, conspiratorially. "I wouldn't be surprised if he had something to do with it. Maybe he took out Joseph Larkin so he could move in and take all that property."

"Your imagination's getting away from you, Helena," Bert said.

"Besides, you're forgetting the EpiPen," Maggie said. "Someone snuck it out of Mrs Larkin's bag. And unless one of you saw Evans lurking around Sam's restaurant the day Larkin was murdered, it doesn't seem like he would have been able to do it."

"So, you think the EpiPen is the key to all of this?" Jim asked. Although he was trying to suppress it, Maggie could see the old detective in him peeking out, wanting to dive back into the fray and uncover the mystery.

"It's definitely part of it," Maggie said. "We know it had to be premeditated. The fact that someone snuck peanut flour into the kitchen proves that, and the EpiPen going missing is no coincidence."

"We need to find that EpiPen," Kate said.

"That'll be like finding a needle in a haystack," Bert said. "If they were smart at all, then they would have chucked it as soon as they got their hands on it."

"I'll bet it's the wife," Liv said as she tapped the tips of her perfectly manicured nails on her glass. Her voice was hard as steel, and Maggie knew that Liv wanted her husband exonerated more than just about anything. The protectiveness was rather endearing and one of the things Maggie loved about her. "I'd like to give her a piece of my mind about framing an innocent man."

"I'm pretty sure you'll end up doing that to whoever turns out to have done it," Bert said amicably. He took the first sip of a fresh pint, and smacked his lips. Liv didn't argue with him.

Chapter Twelve

THE MOMENT MAGGIE OPENED the front door and saw the excitement on Kate's face, she knew something significant had happened and that Kate had concocted a plan long before ringing her doorbell. Whether it was a good plan or not was yet to be seen.

"What did you do?" Maggie asked, letting her cousin in, who clearly had not even taken the time to change out of her uniform. The cottage yet again smelled of baking biscuits.

"I was talking to Lizzie at the manor today," she said. "She seemed distracted and a little upset, so I asked her what was wrong, and she said she was considering quitting. When I asked why, she seemed unwilling to talk about it. She said she was worried I might get in trouble. When I told her I couldn't care less, she still refused."

"Well, I don't blame her. But what does this have to do with you coming over spur-of-the-moment like this?"

"Well…" Kate said, drawing out the word. It was the type of 'well' that Kate used when she'd decided to execute a plan but had conveniently forgotten to tell people the plan involved them. Based on the look in Kate's eyes, that plan involved Maggie.

"Whatever it is—" Maggie began, before Kate interrupted her.

"I haven't even told you what it is I'm thinking. You can't say 'no' until you've heard me out."

"I'm not sure why you find her being cagey so suspicious. She might just not enjoy her job and be thinking of leaving. There's nothing untoward about that."

"But there was something in the way she said it, a kind of fear, perhaps. And I knew that I had to find out more," Kate said.

"So just ask her."

"I can't. I'm too close to the whole thing. I'm really not sure if she trusts me. She worries that if she tells me then it will get out to someone in the manor. Mr Lawrence or Mrs Larkin, perhaps. What we need is someone who is not employed by the manor, someone who doesn't have a stake in this whole thing."

Maggie thought for a moment and dismissed all members of the MBC almost as soon as she had thought of them. They would be too unsubtle and give the game away.

"And who would that be?" But based on the look on Kate's face, Maggie knew perfectly well who her cousin had in mind: her.

"Perhaps," said Kate, "someone with some experience in psychology and therapy and stuff." When Maggie shot Kate a glare. "You've read books! And you took a psychology module at uni."

"Just because I've read a few books doesn't make me qualified to draw out secrets from strangers."

"Well, I can't do it. It's just too suspicious when I ask her so many questions whenever I bump into her. You are the only person in the whole of Sandy Cove who can pull it off. You are personable and caring and a fantastic listener, I've always thought that." She was laying it on a bit thick now, but Maggie still couldn't help but feel a little flattered. She could see the excitement on her cousin's face and had already calculated that if they kept arguing Kate would just win her around in the end, so she skipped that part and just cut to the chase.

Maggie sighed and shook her head in quiet astonishment. "When's the meeting?"

"I wanted to ask you first, to check your diary and see if you're free..." She couldn't keep up the pretence any longer. "Tomorrow at noon," she announced, followed by a sheepish grin.

All Maggie could do was laugh. It was almost impossible to ever be annoyed at Kate, which made it even more difficult to say no. At the moment that the oven timer sounded, Maggie wondered where she had stashed her old psychology books. Maybe it wouldn't hurt to do a little revision.

~~~

Having smuggled Maggie back into the mansion, Kate found an excuse to leave her alone with Lizzie in the staff break room. This was not something Maggie had agreed to, but before Maggie could grab her, Kate had hurried away, mumbling something about needing to locate a mop on the second floor.

Now alone with Lizzie, who was idly leafing through a magazine, Maggie cleared her throat and turned towards her.

"Kate said you wanted to talk?" she asked, trying to adopt a comforting expression.

Lizzie looked up at her.

"Who, me?"

"Yes," Maggie said.

Her face reddened a little. "That girl is really quite persistent," Lizzie said.

Maggie laughed. "No kidding. One Christmas when she was a kid, she was so determined to find out what Santa would bring her for Christmas that she not only stayed up all night, but she tried to install a camera in the chimney to see how he climbed down."

Lizzie giggled. "I haven't known her very long, but I can definitely see her doing that. Why does it always feel like she's up to something?"

"She's just full of energy," said Maggie, trying to play down the fact that she *was* up to something. "She's always been like that."

She closed the magazine and lowered her voice.

"What has she been saying about me?"

Maggie didn't want to make it sound like they had been gossiping about her.

"Nothing. She was just worried that you weren't enjoying your job."

Lizzie appeared slightly uncomfortable, indicating her displeasure at how easily she could be read.

"I can't do this job forever. I've got to leave sometime and maybe I shouldn't keep delaying the inevitable. I think it's time."

Maggie could sense that there was more to the story than the housekeeper was telling. She considered her options. She wanted to know more, but if she went about it the wrong way, Lizzie would clam up and Maggie would never get another word out of her. She needed to choose her words carefully. If she could get her to open up a bit first, then maybe she'd be able to get the information she was searching for.

"I'm sure you'll be missed," Maggie said.

Lizzie laughed and shook her head. "Maybe some of the other staff would be missed, but they wouldn't miss me."

"What about Mrs Larkin? If you're looking after the house, I'm sure she doesn't want to lose you."

Lizzie stiffened and glanced at the door. Her hazel eyes suddenly looked wary and apprehensive, as though worried someone was going to barge into the room at any minute. Just her reaction alone was enough to put Maggie on edge.

"I could really use some fresh air," Lizzie said. "Do you want to go on a walk?"

"That would be lovely," said Maggie. She couldn't wait to get out of this house.

A few minutes later, the two of them were out on the sprawling lawn. The sun was beating down heavily, and the first prickles of sweat began to rise on the back of Maggie's neck. The roar of the ocean as it hit the cliffs was audible in the distance as the wind whipped their hair away from their faces.

Lizzie sighed and took a deep lungful of air. "I'm always afraid Mrs Larkin is going to walk into the room and hear me saying something about her."

"What are you so worried about her overhearing?" Maggie asked.

"It's terrible here," she said, so bluntly it took Maggie by surprise. Though the girl still glanced over her shoulder again, as if worried someone could overhear, even as Maggie herself could barely hear her over the wind. "I would miss some of the staff, like Chris and your cousin. But Mrs Larkin? Not a chance. She's been a nightmare ever since Mr Larkin died. I thought she would soften a little, but if anything, she has become worse. She's turned into an absolute tyrant in her own house."

"Why did you think it would get better after Mr Larkin died?" she asked. "If it was so terrible, why didn't you leave?"

"Because he wouldn't let me," Lizzie said. "I tried to hand in my notice and he just tore it up, said I wouldn't work in Sandy Cove again if I left him. He knew my parents lived here and that I was supporting them. My dad is sick and I couldn't risk having to leave Sandy Cove, so I just kept going."

"Why was he so adamant that you stick around?"

Lizzie didn't answer, but her cheeks turned a brilliant red as she stared down at her feet. And then Maggie remembered what Kate had said about how creepy Larkin had been when she had worked down on the beach whenever she was in a bikini. A chill ran through her.

"Did Larkin make a pass at you?" Maggie asked carefully. "Is that why you wanted to leave in the first place?"

"He tried," Lizzie said. "But after the first time, I made sure to never be in the room alone with him."

"I'm so sorry," Maggie said. "That's terrible. Did you try to tell Mrs Larkin?"

Lizzie shrugged. "The last girl who did that got fired," she said. "Mrs Larkin doesn't like the implication that her husband would even think of cheating on her. Especially with a member of staff."

There was a bitter note of irony to her words that piqued Maggie's interest. But before she could ask more about it, Lizzie had shaken her head as though to clear it. She sighed and closed her eyes.

"I'm sorry," she said. "But I can't talk much more right now. I need to get back in before she or Mr Lawrence come looking for me."

Maggie knew when not to push too far. "Of course," she said. "Let me walk you back. I need to go say bye to Kate before leaving."

The two walked back to the large house in silence. More than anything, Maggie wanted to probe further into what had happened. The more she learned, the more it seemed there were some suspicious goings on at the manor that might shed light on what was truly happening. But it was also obvious that asking Lizzie about it, especially now, was not the best option. The closer they got to the house, the more timid and reserved the housekeeper seemed to get. The contrast between the way she had acted out in the yard and the way she was behaving now that they were re-entering the house made it feel like she turned into a different person as soon as she stepped over the threshold.

When they reached the door to the kitchen, Maggie held it open for Lizzie, who hurried off without another word, leaving Maggie in the doorway. Chris, over at the stove, glanced up and watched the younger woman scurry off as garlic and mushrooms sizzled in his pan and filled the room with tantalisingly savoury scents that made Maggie's mouth water.

"Everything all right?" he asked, looking over at the door through which Lizzie had disappeared.

"I hope so." Mercifully, Maggie was saved from having to answer any further questions by Kate's fortuitous arrival. Her cousin's eyes locked on her as soon as she stepped into the room. Before Maggie could say or do anything, Kate beckoned her over and pulled her into an empty room.

"What did she say?" Kate asked in a hushed voice. Maggie relayed everything Lizzie had told her. "I always said he was a creep," Kate said. "Poor Lizzie. And I can't blame her for not liking Mrs Larkin. She's so demanding. I can barely stand her myself. One time she had me remake her tea four times. I did it the same way each time! If I wasn't trying to solve a murder, I'd leave immediately."

"Considering that's the only reason you took the job in the first place, that isn't saying a whole lot."

A scream cut through the house, disturbing the silence. Kate and Maggie both jumped, their eyes wide with fear. Another attack? But it hadn't quite sounded like a scream of fear. Rather it had sounded like one of vehement indignation. Kate and Maggie's heads swung towards the open door and the sound of pounding footsteps that were quickly approaching them. Hurriedly, Kate pulled Maggie into a corner, and the two of them watched as Amélie Larkin stormed past the doorway. Her fingers were tapping her phone screen furiously, and she looked like a woman on the warpath who would murder anyone who got in her way.

They quietly approached the doorway and watched her as she walked along the corridor and disappeared out of sight. Kate and Maggie looked at one another.

"I wonder what got her so upset," Maggie said.

Kate's eyes sparkled and she looked the other way down the corridor and towards the door of Mrs Larkin's study. She looked at Maggie and smiled. "Want to find out?"

A wave of fear ran through Maggie, but she closed her eyes and took a breath. If Kate was going to step one foot into that study, it was her duty as a cousin to ensure that she didn't do it alone.

They walked as quietly and as quickly as they could along the corridor. When Kate took hold of the door handle, Maggie was certain it was going to be locked. If anything, she was relieved that their scheme had ended before it had begun, but when Kate turned the handle and pushed the door open, Maggie knew there was no turning back.

Amélie Larkin's study was as grand and fancy as the rest of the house, steeped in its Georgian heritage with high ceilings and rich woodwork. The oak desk in front of the tall windows looked as though it were more expensive than Maggie's entire cottage. She scanned the room, taking in the stunning artwork, the gorgeous vases and leather-bound books. There was a wine cabinet in one corner filled with a variety of dusty wines, most of which were no less than twenty years old.

The desk was cluttered with various documents. One had fallen to the floor and was resting on the burgundy rug. Maggie picked it up and began to read.

"This is a bank statement," Maggie said softly. She placed the page back on the ground exactly where she found it. "Kate, I don't think we should be reading this."

Naturally, Kate, being the responsible adult that she was, picked up the paper herself and began reading it. At the look Maggie gave her, Kate shrugged and grinned, saying, "What? I figure we needed a second opinion on how bad it was." Then she returned to scanning the paper. Her eyebrows slowly rose as if it contained the juiciest piece of gossip she had ever read. "Interesting," she said. "Do you see all these massive transfers?"

Maggie's curiosity won out, and she began scanning the document too. "Interesting," she said. "They're all to the same bank account. Do you think she's being blackmailed or something? Or do you think this is what she was so upset about just now?"

"There's definitely something going on here," Maggie said.

"And you know..." Kate said contemplatively. "In all the fuss and excitement, I've completely forgotten to clean this room. I should really get on that. I don't want to be accused of being neglectful."

"Yes..." Maggie said, side-eyeing her cousin with fond exasperation. "That would be terrible. Does that include cleaning out the drawers?"

"Naturally."

"Well, I'm already here, I may as well help you with your job. We can't have you getting in trouble now, can we?"

"I knew you'd want to help out poor Mrs Larkin."

"Yes, I don't know how she copes with only two housekeepers, poor thing."

The two began 'cleaning,' opening drawers and cabinets and giving them a cursory look before hurriedly closing them again. Maggie tentatively approached the desk.

She opened and shut each of the drawers in turn, but when she slid open the middle drawer on the left side, she froze. Her eyes widened.

"Kate..." she said. And the tone in her voice was enough to make the other woman halt her own search and hurry over. She stopped when she saw the contents, her face a mirror of Maggie's own.

"Oh," she said softly. "That...wasn't what I was expecting."

Tucked away in the back of the drawer, nearly out of sight, was an EpiPen.

"It could have been a spare?" Maggie said.

"But why would she have a spare hidden at the back of her desk in her office, where the odds of Joseph Larkin eating peanuts is a million-to-one?"

Maggie shrugged. "It's a possibility," she said. "We can't rule it out. But we need to take this to Tom."

By the time Kate nodded, Maggie was already pulling out her phone and taking a photo of the EpiPen. Once she was done, she stuffed her phone back in her pocket and said, "Let's go to Tom tomorrow after your shift."

They had snuck out of the office, closing the door softly behind them. But they had no sooner done so than heavy footsteps echoed through the house, growing louder as they came closer.

Before Maggie could even fully react, Kate flung open the linen closet, reaching up to grab the sheets on the top shelf. The door blocked Maggie's view of the rest of the hall, but it wasn't hard to guess who was coming towards them. Her suspicions were confirmed when Kate said, "Mr Lawrence. Is there something I can help you with?"

"I heard noises coming from this area," Lawrence said. "You do realise that Mrs Larkin's office is strictly off limits?"

"Of course," Kate said. Her voice was unnaturally, almost sarcastically bubbly. "I was just grabbing some linens. I wouldn't dream of going in there."

"I see. And the fact that your cousin is currently with you is a coincidence?"

Maggie winced, heat flooding up her entire face. How was she this incompetent at hiding? She stepped away from the cupboard to find Mr Lawrence staring sternly at her.

"She's just here because I needed a change of uniform," Kate said.

"In that case, there's no reason for her to stay here." Lawrence was unsmiling, while Kate's smile faltered. It was clear she wasn't used to people being immune to her charm. "Shall I escort her out?"

Maggie went without an argument. As they walked towards the exit, Lawrence said, "I would appreciate it if you stopped coming around so frequently, Miss Treloar. It seems you're distracting your cousin from her job, and if it continues, I'm going to have no choice but to let her go."

Losing this job would matter to Kate about as much as missing out on a salad special at a vegan restaurant. But it was probably best not to say that, so she kept her mouth shut. Still, his gaze burned into her back the entire time she walked to her car, and it wasn't until she was driving away that he retreated into the manor and locked the front door.

Chapter Thirteen

DI TOM PEARCE LOOKED at the photo of the EpiPen as Constable Matthew Brown hovered over his shoulder and stared intently, his eyes wide with boyish interest. Tom looked up at Maggie, his lips a thin line, as he arched an eyebrow.

"And you had probable cause to search Mrs Larkin's drawers?" he asked.

"I was tidying up," Kate said. "It is part of my job. Maggie just happened to be visiting at the time. When I saw this, I knew that I needed to bring it to you."

"Of course." Tom glanced down at his lap, where Biscuit had just rested her head. She looked up at him with an earnest expression, her tail wagging slowly and hopefully. His expression softened, and he scratched the Cavapoo's head, instantly doubling the speed of her tail.

"Ladies," he said, handing Maggie back her phone. She tried not to notice that their fingers brushed up against one another. "While I appreciate the enthusiasm and zeal, you can't keep doing these things. It risks hindering the police investigation. Think about it this way: if you had gone about this discovery inappropriately, I wouldn't have been able to use it as evidence. Thankfully it shouldn't be an issue this time, but one wrong step and the defence will easily be able to get the trial thrown out of court."

"So, you're just going to ignore this?" Kate asked, gesturing towards Maggie's phone.

"I didn't say that," Tom said. He sighed and mussed his hair, pushing the brown locks away from his forehead. "I'm simply asking you to be careful. And not just because you could affect evidence gathering. In case you've forgotten, there's a killer on the loose, and if we're not careful, then there's a chance they might see you as a threat, and therefore a target. And I'd prefer not to see either of your bodies showing up in the mortuary."

Kate and Maggie didn't say anything for a moment, as if contemplating the likelihood of that outcome. Eventually, Maggie asked, "What have you learned about the peanut flour?"

"A little," he said, "but we're still looking into it."

He didn't elaborate, instead taking the opportunity to look down and scratch Biscuit behind the ears, as though the conversation had fully concluded. Maggie tried to refrain from huffing in irritation.

"Could you at least tell us the brand?" Maggie asked. Any sliver of information could be useful enough for them to unravel the mystery themselves.

Tom gave her a look, then relented. "It's called Presidential Flour, some gourmet American brand that's nearly impossible to find in the UK."

"Is that all you're going to tell us?" Kate asked, actually giving a piteous pout in hopes that he would relent. Tom simply stared, stony faced, her charms clearly wasted on the senior detective. "So, what are you going to do with the information we gave you?" she asked.

"Follow up on it, of course." Tom stood and stretched, much to the vexation of Biscuit, whose scratches were now interrupted.

~~~

"I know you love baking," Kate said, kicking her feet up on the dashboard. "But do you need to bring an entire spread up to the manor?"

"You're one to talk," Maggie said. "I know you love my car, but do you need me to drive you up here when you have a perfectly good one?"

"Touché. My argument still stands, though."

"We should at least pretend I'm not there only to eavesdrop on Tom and Mrs Larkin," Maggie said, looking down at the tin of biscuits resting on the back seat. Biscuit the Cavapoo was sitting next to it, her nose pressed against the metal and staring pitifully at it as if begging for the tin to magically open and offer up the goodies inside. "If I'm just wandering around, it's going to look suspicious. At least if I go to store biscuits in the kitchen, I have an excuse to be inside the house." She didn't add that she fully intended to hook Chris into another conversation about baking, though she doubted she would get his full attention, not with the kind of tunnel vision he has when cooking.

"If you say so," Kate said. "Though I'm fairly certain Tom isn't going to fall for it."

Maggie didn't respond. Instead, she came to a stop in the driveway and clambered out, being sure to grab her Cavapoo and the biscuits before heading around the mansion.

When she stepped into the grand kitchen, Chris was crouched in the pantry, clutching a clipboard and counting under his breath as he made notes. He glanced up when he heard her enter.

"Hello," he said. "Your cousin forgot her lunch again?"

"I was her lift," Maggie said, then held up the small tin. "Though I definitely didn't expect to be her packhorse as well. She was too lazy to bring her food to the kitchen."

Chris gave a *heh* of amusement, though didn't drag himself away from his inventory. "That's always fun," he said. "Gotta love lazy relatives."

Maggie opened the tin, "I'm taking a biscuit tax for my troubles," she announced. Kate only asked me to bring the tin into the kitchen. She didn't say anything about me not eating any of them. Would you like one?"

Chris shrugged, then, to her surprise, put down his clipboard and strolled over. He picked up one of the homemade Hobnobs, a golden oat biscuit, dipped in chocolate, and bit into it.

"These were always my favourite," he said after he swallowed.

"You know, I was thinking of trying something different," Maggie said, sudden inspiration hitting her like a freight train. "My friend is gluten free and loves peanut butter. I was thinking of trying to make some biscuits with peanut flour instead of all-purpose. Do you know anything about that?"

"Not much," he said. "It works a bit differently, I think. And it's good for bread, and keto diets and such, if you're looking for a non-gluten alternative."

"Do you know of any good brands?" Maggie asked. "I've been looking into it. I found this one type from Presidential Flour, and it looks—"

Chris broke her off, laughing hysterically. "Sorry," he said, "but Presidential Flour is a con. Have you seen the prices they charge? Their entire range—bread, all-purpose, self-rising—is absurdly expensive. I have friends who are chefs and we all make fun of Presidential Flour, and of anyone who goes to the effort of importing it in. You'd have to be ridiculously wealthy, and remarkably gullible, to even get hold of it in the UK. The only way to get your hands on it is to ship it across the pond."

Maggie pulled out her phone and quickly looked it up.

"Oh," she said, staring at the prices. "Wow."

Chris nodded. "Besides, most peanut flour is the same," he said. "It's just ground and defatted peanuts. You could get away even with using peanut powder, I bet. A lot easier to get your hands on. You'll just need to adjust the sugar and salt ratios. Do not waste your time with Presidential. Just save your money."

"Thanks." Maggie glanced over at him as she noticed something. "Are you originally from Cornwall?"

Chris blinked and cocked his head. "Accent give it away?" he asked. "I've tried hard to get rid of it, but the closer I get to home, the stronger it gets."

"It's fairly strong," she admitted. "It's just your knife roll has the name Tredinnick on it. It's a very Cornish name."

Chris nodded, seemingly a little unnerved. "Yeah, I grew up in the area," he said. "But my family moved to just outside London when I was a teenager. One of the reasons I like working for the Larkins is that I get to come back here. On my days off, I can surf or fish. It's nice. Makes me feel close to my dad."

"That sounds nice," Maggie said.

The door to the rest of the house banged open and Kate hurried in.

"Maggie," she said. "Would you mind helping me with something?" She stared meaningfully at the tin of biscuits with an unspoken *And bring that with you.*

"Thanks for all your advice," Maggie said, taking the tin and closing it.

"Any time," he replied. "Always happy to talk shop." Then he picked up his clipboard and returned to the pantry to finish his inventory.

"Let me guess," Maggie said, holding up the tin. "Bribery?"

"Of course," Kate said, "what else?"

Maggie rolled her eyes, but couldn't hold back her smile.

As they walked down the corridor that led to the closed door of Amélie Larkin's study, they could hear her raised voice quite clearly.

"Are you mad?" Amélie asked, clearly outraged. "Why would I hold on to such an incriminating piece of evidence? What do you take me for, an idiot?"

"I don't think you're an idiot, Mrs Larkin," Tom said. "But there is an EpiPen in your drawer. And you're saying you have no idea how it got there? You don't keep it there as a spare?"

"If I kept it there as a spare," Amélie said, her voice dripping with venom, "don't you think I would have told you as much?"

"I would certainly hope so," Tom said, though in a far calmer tone and at a far more reasonable volume. "But we have to check these things out."

The voices lowered some, becoming indistinguishable murmurs. Kate and Maggie looked at one another, then hurried closer to the shut door. They crouched down, placing their ears against the oak in the hopes of being able to hear them. Biscuit scooted along the wall, imitating her owner's strange behaviour. Maggie's heart pounded with excitement and nerves.

"Who told you, anyway?" Amélie asked. "Was it one of the staff? Tell me so I can fire them."

"We're not going to divulge our sources, Mrs Larkin," Matthew said, chiming in.

Kate suppressed a giggle, and Maggie understood why. Matthew actually keeping his mouth shut must have been a first for him. But that didn't stop Maggie from nudging her cousin in the shin and making a frantic shushing motion to try and get her to quiet down. Kate paled momentarily at the realization she might have given them away, then relaxed when there was no audible reaction coming from the other side of the door.

"You should be putting more effort into looking into my bank accounts," she said. "Someone has been funnelling money from my account to a separate account I've never heard of before. You should prioritise that."

"That's for the fraud department to investigate, Mrs Larkin," Matthew said. "Rest assured we're working with them to get to the bottom of this."

"I'm glad you decided not to mention that part," Kate whispered to Maggie. She nodded. They had agreed before going to speak to Tom that seeing someone's bank statements was a little too dicey, and that, unless it became relevant or it seemed Tom wouldn't learn of it on his own, they would keep that fact to themselves. It seemed as though Amélie had informed them at some point.

"Now, I'm just covering my bases," Tom said, cautiously, "but you are certain that these transactions are fraudulent?"

His placating tone did not do what it had set out to achieve.

Amélie Larkin exploded.

"How dare you," she shouted. "Are you implying that I would be stealing from myself? Or maybe you assume that I'm so financially incompetent that I wouldn't remember transfers of hundreds of thousands of dollars to the exact same account? Or maybe you think I'm bribing someone or being blackmailed?"

"Mrs Larkin—" Tom began. But she was building up steam and it was clear that her tirade wasn't about to be quelled any time soon.

"It's my husband's doing, I know it is. You have no idea how financially irresponsible that oaf was. I don't know why I married him in the first place. All he was after was my money. If it weren't for the prenup he would have divorced me ages ago. Not that I would have minded. I should have pulled the trigger on that a decade ago, but I detest scandal. Have you looked at *his* bank accounts? He was nearly broke. Bad investment after bad investment. I'll bet he was the one who managed to worm his way into my accounts to funnel the money… to himself. Last time I'm that stupid. I've already fired my financial manager and my accountant. It's impossible to get good help these days. I have half a mind to sue them, and don't get me started on—"

The echoes of Amelie's tirade subsided into nothingness, as if she realized that she was digging herself into a hole and Tom was letting her. There was a long, uncomfortable pause, and Maggie panicked momentarily, wondering if Mrs Larkin was about to storm outside and they would be caught.

"I understand you're upset," Tom said, and Maggie relaxed. "Rest assured, we are looking into everything, including your husband's bank accounts. But this is a matter of due diligence. We have to ask these questions. They don't mean we suspect you of any wrongdoing. You have to understand that."

There was silence when he finished. Then small sniffles. Maggie and Kate exchanged dumbfounded glances. Was Amélie Larkin *crying*?

"I know you've been under a great deal of stress," Tom said, his voice softer and more understanding. "But you need to understand that we're trying to do our job. Besides your husband, is there anyone else you can think of that might be responsible for stealing your money?"

"Why don't you ask George Evans?" she said.

Maggie's eyes widened. She looked at Kate, whose mouth had dropped open in shock. They exchanged dumbfounded glances.

"George Evans?" Even Tom sounded surprised. "Why would George Evans have anything to do with your bank account? And how would he have access to your funds?"

"Joseph owed him thousands," Amélie said. "For all I know, Joseph funnelled the money to him as payment."

"So George Evans wouldn't know that the money had actually come from you?"

"How should I know?" Amélie asked.

"Why would you suggest Mr Evans? I'm only trying to—"

"I want you out of here," Amélie said sternly, her voice regaining that harsh edge. "I want you out, and the next time you want to talk to me, my lawyer will be present, do you understand?"

"Of course," Tom said. "Thank you for your time."

Maggie and Kate's eyes flew wide with alarm, and both of them scrambled backward, to avoid the door swinging open. Even Biscuit scooted back, her tail thumping eagerly as if she thought it was a game.

Just before the door opened fully, Kate hauled Maggie to her feet and scurried in the direction of the linen closet. But it was too late. Tom's eyes found Maggie. His posture tensed and his jaw twitched. The annoyance in his eyes made Maggie shrivel to the size of a peanut. At first, she thought he would scold them right there. But he said nothing, and instead jerked his head to indicate they should talk elsewhere.

But before Maggie could follow his directions, she froze as another figure strolled out after the two officers.

"Allow me to escort you gentlemen out to your car," Mr Lawrence said. Maggie tried to hide herself, backing up against the wall.

"That won't be necessary," Tom said. "We can find our own way out."

"I insist," Mr Lawrence said. Then, as if there were a radar in his head, he looked directly at Kate and Maggie who, in a panic, had failed to be very good at hiding. He marched towards them.

"I thought I had made it clear that you are not to show up unannounced anymore. This is not her house," he said, pointing sharply at Kate. "And you, Miss Edwards, are not free to invite guests to come and go willy-nilly."

"She forgot her lunch again," Maggie said hurriedly, knowing full well that this excuse was wearing very thin. She could feel Tom's eyes boring into her from along the corridor, but she kept her gaze locked on Lawrence. "I was just bringing it by for her."

"In which case, you should have delivered it to the kitchen and left."

"That's what I was going to do. I just wanted to say bye to Kate first."

"And have you?" There was no amusement or friendliness in his expression. In fact, something about his indifferent demeanour made Maggie certain that you'd find barely contained rage behind it.

"Uh, yes," she said. "Bye, Kate."

"I'll see her out, Mr Lawrence," Kate said hurriedly. "And the officers as well."

Maggie thought that Lawrence might protest, but he seemed tired of dealing with them. "Very well. I have other things to do. Just make sure they actually leave. Now." Walking off, it looked to be the end of it. But then Lawrence paused and turned back around. "Oh, and Miss Treloar," he said. "If I see you again loitering on the property without good cause, I will consider it trespassing and it will be you who the police will be talking to."

And then he retreated along the corridor.

"Well?" Tom asked, when they were all outside in the drive. "Did you hear everything you wanted?"

"A confession would have been nice," Kate said, completely unfazed by the encounter with Lawrence, and by the fact she had been openly eavesdropping on police business. "But I'll take what I can get."

Maggie elbowed Kate, glaring. The look in Tom's eyes told her he wasn't exactly in the mood for levity, and she didn't want to try his patience. "I'm going to ignore the eavesdropping this time," he said. "But it's not exactly a habit I approve of when it comes to active police investigations. There is such a thing as confidential information, you know."

"You're right," Maggie said. "I'm sorry. We were just curious."

To prevent any more questionable comments from Kate, Maggie opened the biscuit tin and held it out towards the two officers. Matthew's hand shot out eagerly and grabbed the first thing his fingers came to: a Cornish Fairing. Tom, almost reluctantly, peered inside.

"Are any of these your favourites?" Maggie asked. "I wasn't joking when I said I would figure it out."

Tom smirked, his eyes sparkling as he picked out a chocolate Hobnob. He held it up towards the sun, squinting as if he were scrutinising it to look for flaws. Then he bit into it.

"Delicious," he said. "But not my favourite. Anything that involves oats is going to be mid-tier for me. Though the chocolate improves it."

"Noted," Maggie said. Already she was calculating in her head: not ginger, not oats, at least partial to chocolate in some capacity. At this point, she had made it her mission to figure out this mystery as though it were another case to solve. She was about to close the tin, but Matthew quickly grabbed a Hobnob of his own.

"Unlike my superior," Matthew said cheerily, his mouth full, "I don't discriminate against oats."

"We can't all be such paragons of virtue," Tom said. "Do I want to know why the steward seems to think you're around too often, Maggie? That seemed like quite the reaction from him."

"Have another biscuit." Maggie thrust the tin at him. He gave her an annoyed look before sticking his hand in the tin and pulling out another hobnob.

"Do you really think George Evans might have had something to do with all of this?" she asked. The more she got off the topic of Lawrence, the better.

Thankfully, the detective inspector didn't seem to feel the need to press further. He shrugged. "That's something for us to figure out." He glanced at his phone. "We've got to get going. I'm certain we'll see you around."

Maggie, Kate, and Biscuit watched as the two men drove off.

"Well," Kate said. "It's certainly been a rather interesting day, hasn't it?"

Maggie nodded her agreement.

"Do you think I could hold on to the rest of the biscuits?" Kate asked. "They're perfect for afternoon tea."

"I think I'll survive if you feel it absolutely necessary."

"I do," Kate said gravely. Then the two burst into giggles.

Maggie walked Kate back along the outside of the house towards the kitchen. She glanced in the windows, admiring the stunning rooms inside. How many rooms did this house have? But all thoughts of that came to a screeching halt when she glanced inside what might have been a library.

Amélie Larkin and Peter were standing inside. Peter's hands were resting on her shoulders, and he was bending down to talk to her softly. Their faces were inches apart. Then, even as Maggie watched, Peter pulled her close and enveloped her in a hug. His hand patted the back of Mrs Larkin's head reassuringly.

Before Maggie could fully process just what she had seen, the two had broken apart and moved away from the window and out of sight, and Maggie partially wondered if she had seen it at all.

Chapter Fourteen

"THINGS ARE DEFINITELY DEVELOPING, aren't they, Biscuit?" Maggie asked, as she began rolling out the biscuit dough. "I've been starting to think more and more about George Evans. If we listen to Mrs Larkin, it appears her husband had some sort of business arrangement with him. Or at the very least, it seems like she thinks he owed Evans money. Granted, it could have absolutely nothing to do with real estate. It could have been a gambling debt, for all I know. But considering they're in the same industry, I'm guessing it has to do with some sort of partnership or business-related loan. What do you think?"

Biscuit cocked her head as she listened to Maggie, her ruby-coloured tail swishing along the floor as it thumped against the cabinet.

Maggie leaned against the counter and drummed her fingers as another thought occurred to her. "Do you remember what Kate said about it looking like items were missing? And Lizzie apparently confirming it? What if Larkin was stealing them to pay off whatever debt he had? And when it wasn't enough, he started stealing his wife's money? That could make sense, couldn't it?"

Biscuit huffed.

"And then there's Peter and Amélie," Maggie said as she pulled out an elegant biscuit cutter. She expertly began punching out the biscuits and moving them delicately onto the trays. "Though I don't know what to make of that. There's clearly something going on there. Kate said she'd keep an eye out, though. So I guess we'll find out something about that sooner or later."

"I wonder who else has been contacted by George Evans," Maggie said. She drummed her fingers against the counter, silver biscuit cutter still in the other hand, dangling from a finger. "Do you think it's the same people Joseph Larkin talked to?"

Biscuit made a soft *woof*, though considering her eyes were on the ball of dough Maggie was currently popping into her mouth, Maggie guessed it had more to do with wanting biscuits than commentary on the mystery.

"Humans can have raw dough," Maggie said, rolling another discarded fragment into a ball and eating it. "Dogs can't."

Biscuit whined and lowered her head to the floor.

"I'd say the next step is to see who else George Evans reached out to," Maggie said contemplatively as she put the cut-out dough into the fridge to chill for an hour. "And we should probably start with the one closest to home."

~~~

"He did reach out, actually," June said as she swept the floor before opening that day. "He sent me an email about a week ago. I just ignored it."

"You don't think that was weird, considering Joseph Larkin was interested only a few days before that?" Maggie asked.

June shrugged. "I didn't see how it made much difference who reached out," she said. "The answer was always going to be no."

Maggie nodded, patting Biscuit absentmindedly as her mind wandered. If George Evans had contacted both Abigail and June, she wondered who else he might have gotten in touch with that had been on Larkin's radar as well.

"Do you know if Sam's had any messages from him?" she asked.

"I'm fairly certain that Sam has more pressing things on his mind right now than a real estate investor sniffing around, especially one who didn't die on his property," June said. "So no, he hasn't told me anything."

"Do you know anything about him?" Maggie asked.

"The same as anyone else. It isn't as though he comes here for tea or anything."

Maggie let out a small huff of frustration, then tried to look innocent when June shot her a look.

"Do you need me in the shop this afternoon?" Maggie asked, trying to sound casual.

"Why?" June asked. "Are you not feeling well?"

"I've just got a lot on my mind," Maggie said. "I think a walk would help clear my head a bit. And Biscuit could use a walk too."

June eyed her suspiciously but then relented. "If you want," she said. "It's pretty quiet here today."

Biscuit, who had leapt up eagerly at the word 'walk', was already at the door, staring up at Maggie expectantly, her tail wagging as she panted excitedly. Maggie put on Biscuit's harness, clipped the lead to it, and walked outside, waving back at June as she did.

The sun was beating down today, making it unusually hot, even for this time of year. Maggie already had a plan. She was going to talk to Sam, to see if George Evans had spoken to him as well. She had kept it from June because she had guessed her aunt would disapprove of her bothering Sam with these types of questions when he was undoubtedly stressed out about the Larkin murder. But she had to know.

She walked through the winding streets, enjoying the shade the stone buildings provided and taking her time, allowing Biscuit to dictate the pace. When they finally arrived at the restaurant, Maggie paused, a little surprised by what she found.

Normally around lunch, the building was buzzing with the chatter of patrons and the bustle of waiters and waitresses running around trying to take care of all the customers. Today, it was far more subdued. Maybe five or six of the tables were filled, less than half the norm. Maggie frowned at the sight.

She saw Sam wandering through the tables, and his eyes landed on her. He gave a tired grin and a wave as he manoeuvred through the restaurant to get to her.

"Hey, Maggie, are you here for lunch?" he asked hopefully. "Your favourite table is free."

Initially, Maggie had only intended to swing by for a short visit, to see how Sam was doing and to ask about George Evans. But after seeing the state of the restaurant and the meagre number of tables filled, she found herself saying, "Both, actually. Though I'm in a little bit of a hurry."

"No problem. Take a seat and I'll get your usual ready for you," he said, smiling.

True to his word, he was back maybe two minutes later, with a pint of cider in each hand. He placed one in front of her. Another waiter was right behind him with a small water bowl for Biscuit.

"On the house," he said, sitting next to her and taking a sip from his own glass.

"I couldn't," she said hurriedly. If business wasn't going well, which it wasn't, if the lack of patrons was any indication, the last thing she wanted was for Sam to be handing out freebies.

Sam dismissed the protest with a wave of his hand. "Please," he said. "You'd be doing me a favour. I need an excuse of someone to have a drink with. Bert's out of town for the day and he would usually be here letting me get my lunchtime pint in. And I really need it today."

"Are things that bad?" Maggie asked, taking a sip. She couldn't deny that the crisp apple flavour was incredibly refreshing on such a warm day.

He gave a bitter smile to his drink. "It hasn't been great since Larkin died," he said. "Word gets around. I'm pretty sure his wife had something to do with that. I'm sure once the fuss dies down, it'll be fine. Assuming I'm not arrested, that is."

"That's not going to happen," Maggie said firmly. She was surprised by the steel in her voice. "I won't let it."

"I hope you're right. But we'll see." Sam looked around at the restaurant, and it was impossible not to notice the sadness on his face as he looked at how empty it was. "I don't think we've had a lunch this slow during the summer in years. It looks as though Larkin got his wish. Fat load of good it did him."

"It'll pick up," Maggie said firmly. Her food arrived, and it hurt her that it had come out so quickly, when the kitchen should have been backed up with orders at this time of day. "I know it will."

"We'll see," Sam repeated as he took a long sip of cider. "So what did you want to talk about?"

Maggie popped a fry in her mouth, so hot and fresh it nearly burned the roof of her mouth. "I wanted to see if a man named George Evans had contacted you recently," she said after she had swallowed.

"He has," Sam said. "A few days after Larkin's death, actually. He was pretty nice about it. Just swung by, asked if I would be interested in selling. Apparently he owns a few restaurants and high-end bakeries and wanted to expand his collection. I said no, and he gave me his card and told me that if I changed my mind, he'd give me a good price."

"He wasn't rude or anything?" Maggie asked.

"Nah. He was perfectly nice. I didn't think much of it at the time. It's not like I was planning to sell." He sighed, running his fingers through his hair. "Granted, after seeing what Larkin's death is doing to the business, I might have to take him up on it."

He looked crestfallen, and Maggie couldn't blame him. He had worked hard for years to make the fish and chips shop a thriving business. And now he was seeing it all crumble because of an unfortunate event that was entirely beyond his control. It didn't seem fair, and the fact that it was happening at all infuriated her more than she could believe.

She needed to clear Sam's name, if for no other reason than to save the restaurant that had become a beloved staple of Sandy Cove.

"It'll get better once the shock's worn off," Maggie said. "I'm sure of it."

Later, when she had finished eating, she made sure to leave a very generous tip.

As she was walking the long way back to The Book Nook, Biscuit perked up. Her ears twitched, and her head swivelled excitedly to one side as she heard some noise. Then she jerked forward, tugging Maggie along as she darted towards whatever it was she was now bent on tracking.

"Biscuit!" Maggie said, almost laughing. "What are you doing?"

But then they rounded the corner, and she had her answer.

Tom and Matthew were walking down the street. The constable was wearing his uniform, and Tom was in a smart shirt and trousers. They were headed in the direction of the station, probably after a lunch break. Their backs were towards her, but the two men both turned when they heard Biscuit's excited woofs. She barrelled into Matthew and began licking his hands, her tail and butt waggling excitedly.

"Hey there, girl," Matthew said. "How are you today?"

Biscuit, too intent on giving his hands a thorough bath, didn't answer.

"You haven't been eating biscuits, have you?" Maggie asked.

"Guilty," Matthew said. Then his eyes lit up. "In fact..." He fished around in his pocket, before pulling out a plastic bag and holding it up. There was a single fairing inside. "Here you go, girl. They're not as good as Maggie's but I hope you like it."

Biscuit, who didn't care about the origin of any biscuit, liked it just fine, and it was gone in seconds. She turned back to her master. Maggie hadn't thought it was possible for a dog to look smug. But apparently, she was wrong.

"How is the investigation going?" Maggie asked. She tried to sound casual, but apparently she didn't succeed, because Tom gave her an amused look.

"It goes discretely," Tom said, speaking just as Matthew was about to open his mouth. Maggie pursed her lips to hide her amusement. But there was something more pressing on her mind, something she thought Tom and Matthew needed to know, if they didn't already.

"I'm glad I ran into you. I've actually been meaning to talk to you about something," Maggie said. "When I was up at the manor, I saw Mrs Larkin and her handyman in one of the rooms. They seemed rather... well-acquainted. Did you notice that?"

"We did, actually," Matthew said eagerly. "It was something DI Pearce mentioned after we left. Apparently, he noticed it when we first arrived. When Mr Lawrence opened the door for us, Mr Davies wandered out and walked right past us. When we got to Mrs Larkin's office, the DI smelled traces of the cologne Mr Davies had been wearing. I didn't notice it, and of course DI Pearce didn't tell me until later, but..." Matthew trailed off at the withering glare from his superior.

"As I said..." Tom said, glancing back at Maggie, "discretely."

"What about George Evans?" Maggie asked.

That got Tom's attention. He cocked his head, staring intently at Maggie. She could feel herself turning the slightest shade of pink under the scrutiny.

"What about him?" he asked.

"I know Amélie Larkin mentioned him," Maggie said. "But did you know he's been reaching out to all of the businesses Larkin was after?"

The only indication of Tom's surprise was the double blink. "Is that so?" he asked.

Maggie nodded. "He's messaged my aunt and Sam," she said. "And by the way, if you wouldn't mind proving Sam's innocence so people stop boycotting his restaurant, I would appreciate it."

"I'm just doing my job," Tom said. "That doesn't have anything to do with how well his shop is doing."

Maggie stayed silent, staring him down with a stern expression that would have made June proud. Tom glanced away and cleared his throat.

"We're working as fast as we can, Maggie," he said, and something about the tone took Maggie aback. There was a tired sincerity to it, and some of her irritation softened. "We haven't ruled any suspects out yet. But I'm working to get to the bottom of this. As soon as I find out who the killer is, I'll be the first to tell everyone there's no reason to avoid Sam's restaurant. And I am sorry that all of this is causing him problems."

Maggie's muscles loosened a bit. She hadn't realised how tense she was.

"Sorry," she said.

Tom shook his head. "You're worried about a friend. You don't have anything to be sorry about. But don't be so hard on us, either." He checked his watch. "We've got to get back to the station. We'll see you later, Maggie. Thank you for the information on George Evans. We'll be sure to look into it."

With a final pat on Biscuit's head, Tom and Matthew turned and continued walking down the street. Biscuit watched and gave a soft whimper.

"Come on, Biscuit," Maggie said, tugging gently on the dog's lead. "Let's get back to The Book Nook."

As she walked back, her head was filled with thoughts of Sam and George Evans. She knew there had to be some connection between George Evans and the murder—Amélie Larkin had angrily declared as much. But she had no idea what it might be, and she had no proof, only a feeling of certainty in her gut.

She needed to find a way to talk to him. But she had never spoken to the man. She knew him by sight, the same way she knew almost everyone in Sandy Cove. But that was all. She couldn't just waltz up to him and start asking him questions. And he was probably busy. Even if she tried to get an appointment with him, she wouldn't be able to meet with him for months, by which point it would be moot.

The entire time she walked back, she concocted weird and elaborate ways of trying to meet with him. Staging a drowning by jumping in the ocean while he was nearby (uncontrollable), calling, pretending to be an official telling him he had inherited millions of pounds from a previously unknown aunt (unbelievable), or casually running into him on the street and interrogating him (unwise).

But as Maggie opened the door to The Book Nook, she looked over at the man at the counter, and she realised there was no need to do any of that.

George Evans's attention was drawn to the ring of the bell over the door, and his eyes met hers.

Chapter Fifteen

GEORGE EVANS WAS TALL and slim with striking blue eyes. He had a slight paunch that came with age and his hair was grey but in a refined, dignified way. Despite his apparent age, he had very few wrinkles.

The way he held himself made him appear even taller than he might otherwise have been. And the cut of the beautiful suit he was wearing added to his stature. It wasn't showy or ostentatious, but Maggie could tell it was expensive. That was clear in the quality of the material, the nearly invisible stitching, and the way it was tailored to fit him perfectly. It must have cost thousands of pounds.

He studied Maggie briefly, and she felt he was scrutinising her as if trying to decide whether she was worth his time. But then he smiled warmly at her, which felt incongruous with his rather intimidating appearance.

"Hello, Maggie," June said. Her posture was tense and defensive, very much resembling the way she looked the day Larkin had come to see her. Though there was also a hint of annoyance in her eyes as well. It instantly put Maggie on edge.

"Ah, so you're Maggie," he said. He had a northern accent, surprising for a man who spent most of his time in Cornwall, and it took her aback. "Your aunt was just telling me you would be coming back soon. I know we've seen each other around town throughout the years, but I don't know if we've ever been formally introduced. I'm George Evans."

Uncertain, Maggie walked over and shook his outstretched hand. "It's a pleasure to meet you officially, Mr Evans," she said, a little stiffly.

"Please, call me George," he said. "I can't stand formalities when they're not strictly necessary."

"George, then." Maggie glanced over towards her aunt, who was leaning over the counter on her elbows. Her light brown hair was in disarray and a little wild, the way it got when she ran her fingers through her hair, which she only ever did when she was particularly nervous. That protective feeling Maggie sometimes got about her aunt intensified.

"What can we help you with?" Maggie asked. "Looking for something to read?"

She knew he wasn't. There was no chance that was the reason why he was here. But she wanted him to confirm her suspicions rather than her potentially coming off as accusatory or too nosey. Though she was ready to kick him out at a moment's notice if needed.

"Not today," he said. "I had a business proposition for your aunt and wanted to stop by to talk it over with her."

"He was asking me if I wanted to sell," June clarified. "I said no."

Evans chuckled. "I'm not surprised. The Book Nook is such a charming place, and I've seen how busy it can get. I am looking to buy it because I want to protect it. I want to protect the character of Sandy Cove, to ensure it doesn't get taken over by greedy developers with pound signs in their eyes. They don't understand it like I do."

That's funny, thought Maggie, as she had never seen George Evans step foot in the bookshop before.

"You know that Joseph Larkin tried to strong arm June into selling a couple of weeks ago, don't you?" Maggie asked.

He didn't seem very surprised.

"Joseph never did have a soft touch, did he?"

"I heard a rumour that you were business partners..." she said. Out of the corner of her eye, she saw June's eyebrows shoot up, vanishing behind her fringe.

"We were for a time," Evans said, his charm wearing off a little, "but I quickly realised he was not the right partner for me. I was actually in the process of terminating the relationship when he..." Evans trailed off.

"Terminating?" asked Maggie.

"He made a series of bad investments that he didn't consult me on, and started using my money to buy up land—again, without talking to me about it first. The only reason I didn't end it sooner was because I was concerned he would try to find some loophole or exploit in our contract that would mean he wouldn't have to pay me back."

"So he owed you a lot of money?" she asked. When Evans nodded, she asked, "Did you know he was stealing from his wife to pay you?" she asked.

"No," Evans said, shaking his head in bemusement. "If that was the case, I wouldn't be particularly surprised. Joseph was a gambler in more ways than one: he gambled on real estate, in risky business dealings, and in actual casinos too. Honestly, the way he was behaving about the money, taking forever to get it back to me and always weaselling out of our agreed upon repayment plan, I was beginning to wonder how much money he actually had. In all honesty, I had almost given up on getting it back from him."

And now that he's dead, Maggie thought. *What happens? Does he get everything back?* Her pulse quickened. It would be the perfect motive for murder: a jilted business partner conned out of his money finds a way to get it all back through murder.

"Do you get your money from his estate, then?" She made sure her tone was casually curious, perhaps just a touch concerned. She hoped she wasn't pushing her luck.

Evans shrugged. "It's possible, but I'm not particularly optimistic. I'm in the process of discussing the situation with Mrs Larkin."

That explained how Amélie Larkin had figured out about Evans and her suspicions about her money. If he had approached her about the debt, it wouldn't be difficult to guess where her funds had gone.

"But their funds were entirely separate," he said. "Which means if there's no money left in his estate, then I probably won't see a penny of it. But it's just money, and it's not like I haven't made bad investments and lost money before. To me, Joseph was just another bad investment. I don't normally talk ill of the dead like that, but it's how I see it: I took a gamble and it didn't pay off."

"So you're not upset about it?" she asked. "Of course I'm upset about it," Evans said, laughing slightly. "Who wouldn't be? But I'm sure it will all sort itself out."

Considering who his partner had been, George Evans was not what she had expected. He seemed so... cheerful for a man who had lost who knew how much money, but at the same time, he sounded entirely genuine and unbothered by the entire experience. It was not what Maggie had been expecting. There went the motive, she thought.

Before Maggie could question him further, Evans glanced down at his Rolex.

"I'm running a bit late for an appointment," he said. "I'm terribly sorry to leave so abruptly, but I've got to run." He nodded to June. "If you ever wish to sell, June, please reach out. You have my card."

"I'll let you know if I change my mind," June said. "Though don't hold your breath."

Evans smiled and gave a slight nod to the two women before strolling out the door. When he was no longer in sight, June said, "I don't like him."

"Why, was he rude to you?" Maggie asked. "He seemed perfectly nice. Did he offer a low price or something?"

"No," June said, sounding legitimately outraged by his visit. "In fact, he offered me higher than market value."

"So it's purely because he wanted you to sell, and not because he was aggressive or mean about it?"

"I almost wish he had been," June said, again sounding rather frustrated. "At least it would give me a reason for the way I'm feeling. I've just got a bad feeling in my gut. I'm turning into Helena."

"I'm sure you'll find a reason

Maggie fished around in the biscuit jar and pulled out a piece of shortbread. She stared out the window as she munched, considering what she had just learned.

She now had confirmation that Evans and Larkin were business partners. And she knew that Larkin had gambling debts. What if they were going about it all wrong? What if this entire thing had more to do with his debt than anything else? Someone he owed money to finally got fed up with not getting paid. But that didn't make sense. If they killed him, they wouldn't get their money.

"When you've stopped daydreaming," June said, interrupting Maggie's thoughts. "Would you mind doing inventory? There are a lot of gaps on the shelves and I want to find out what's selling. And brew some tea. The MBC is coming over tonight."

Maggie swallowed and nodded, brushing the crumbs away from her mouth, where they fell to the floor in front of the eagerly waiting Biscuit.

"On it," she said.

~~~

Later, after the MBC had gathered and settled down somewhat, Maggie began relaying what she had learned. Yet again, their books—this time *The 7½ Deaths of Evelyn Hardcastle*—lay at their feet, temporarily forgotten.

"Interesting," Liv said. Her perfectly manicured pink nails drummed against her arm as she took all of the information in. "What if it was Amélie? I mean, it sounds as though she had a pretty strong motive. And you said you found an EpiPen in her drawer. To me that feels like fairly substantial evidence."

"Circumstantial, more like," Bert said. "No one's going to convict a woman of murdering her husband over something like that."

"Hmm, I don't know," Helena said. She had recently dyed her hair a vibrant blue. "I just have a feeling. The universe is telling me it's not the wife. Besides, it's too obvious. I mean, it's never the wife in the books; she's always the red herring."

Bert opened his mouth, presumably to remind Helena that this was decidedly *not* a book, when Maggie said, "I'm not sure if it's the wife, but I think they're taking a closer look at all the staff."

"Then why are they still pestering Sam?" Bert asked, jabbing his thumb at Sam, who was currently leaning forward and studying the contents of his teacup. He'd been silent as he listened, clearly still dealing with the after effects of everything. But when June had offered to put a moratorium on the subject, he'd waved her off.

"They're just covering all their bases, Bert," Jim said patiently.

"Easy for a former cop to say," Bert said, grumbling.

"I think they're laying off us," Sam said, sounding tired. "At least a bit. They asked all the kitchen staff a load of questions a few days ago, and they've talked to Senan, my head cook, a handful of times, and myself, obviously. But they haven't been coming around as often. Haven't seen them since they interrogated the staff, and when they talked to me last, it felt a bit perfunctory."

"Well, we can only hope," June said.

The bell above the shop door rang and Kate came bustling in, still in her uniform. Bert choked on his tea when he saw her.

Kate grimaced. "I know, I know. Get over it," she said. "The uniform looks silly. I just didn't have the chance to change."

Kate spotted Helena's change of style. "You dyed your hair again," Kate said. "It's so cute."

"Thank you dear," Helena said, beaming. "It matches my aura better than the red."

Bert laughed under his breath, and June kicked him subtly in the shin.

"Anything exciting happen at work again today?" Maggie asked.

"Nah, everything was normal enough," Kate said. "Peter's as big a flirt as ever."

"What about Chris?" Maggie asked.

"He's still more interested in cooking than life itself."

An idea struck Maggie, and she turned towards Jim. "Chris says he surfs and fishes on his days off. Have you ever seen him?"

Jim scratched his chin as he thought about it. "Couldn't tell you just based on that. I'd need more to go on."

"Young guy, reddish hair. His last name's Tredinnick."

Liv stirred, her brow furrowing.

"I think I know who you're talking about. I've seen him once or twice in the last couple of weeks, ever since the Larkins came for the summer," Jim said. "Not a whole lot, though. I can't imagine he has a load a free time, considering he's employed by Mrs Larkin."

"Do you remember if you saw him there the day Larkin died?"

Jim frowned, scrutinizing his niece as if considering saying something. There was something in his eyes that looked uneasy. Then, he shrugged. "Maybe," he said. "There were a lot of people out that day."

"I saw him," Sam said. All eyes turned to him. "He was surfing. We were there at the same time before I left to catch the lunch rush. He was still there when I left, I'm pretty sure."

"Did you say his name was Tredinnick?" Liv asked.

"Yeah," Maggie said.

"Any relation to Lowen Tredinnick?"

"Who?" Maggie and Kate said in unison, but Bert and Sam looked directly at each other.

"Blimey," Bert said, hand going to his forehead. "Chris is Lowen Tredinnick's son. I remember now. He was a teenager when all that nastiness happened and they moved away."

"Anyone going to clue us in?" Kate asked.

"Lowen Tredinnick had a popular restaurant on Ocean Lane," Liv said. Her eyes sparkled with eagerness at the potential for new evidence. "But Larkin got it shut down. He went into anaphylactic shock after eating peanuts there. Rumour is that Lowen went a bit mad after losing everything, but the family moved away not long after the lawsuit finished."

"His name was Lowen Tredinnick?" Maggie asked, and Helena nodded, eyes sparkling with intrigue at the new revelation "Very nice man, too. He was a Pisces, if I recall."

"So Chris is the son of a man who was ruined by Larkin?" Maggie asked. "It seems weird that he would come back to work for them."

"No kidding," Bert said. "I wonder why he would."

"There has to be a reason," Liv agreed.

"We don't know that," Jim said. "For all we know, this is a huge coincidence."

"Right," Bert said, "and the fish I caught yesterday was as big as Biscuit."

Biscuit looked up at her name, cocking her head. Then, when she realised she wasn't needed, put her head back down and closed her eyes.

"I'm just saying we can't jump to conclusions," Jim said, leaning forward to pour himself more tea.

"And I'm just saying that your inner cop is coming out again, and he's very rational," Bert grumbled. "Let us have our fun."

June, who had been fidgeting over in the corner, finally said, "I'm sorry, but this was a *really* good book, and I've been itching to talk about it for the entire month. Can we put a halt on the real-life mystery for a little while?"

"All right, you heard the lady," Bert said. "We should probably get onto the book before June kicks us out."

June tried to whack him on the arm, but he dodged, grinning widely.

~~~

Later, as things were wrapping up, Jim pulled Maggie and Kate over to one side. His face was surprisingly grim, and his blue eyes were serious. As Bert would have said, his inner cop was showing.

"Girls," he said. "I need to talk to you."

"What's up?" Kate asked.

Jim reached out and gently took both girls by the arm, looking at them levelly, his lips forming a thin line. Biscuit wriggled her way into the small gap between the three of them and looked up curiously.

"This case," Jim said, "I know you want to help Sam, and I'm impressed at everything you've found out. You'd make a good police officer if that would ever interest you, Katie."

Kate wrinkled her nose. "There are too many rules to follow," she replied.

"I know," Jim said, "but those rules are there for a reason. One is to ensure that procedures are followed, and criminals can't get away on a technicality. The other is to protect civilians, people investigating, and officers. Both of which apparently apply to you right now."

Kate held her head high, her chin jutting out in defiance. She brushed away a strand of hair. "You can't make me give up," she said.

"No," he admitted. "And I'm not trying to. You're a grown woman and can make your own decisions, just as you aren't breaking any rules. This isn't me trying to get you to stop, girls. I admire your determination, and I think what you're doing is admirable. This is me telling you I want you to be careful."

"We're not going to break the law," Kate said, "you know that."

"Kate," Jim said. Maggie could hear the sternness in his voice. "This has nothing to do with you breaking the law. I'm sure Tom will step in before it gets to that point. This is me giving you some fatherly advice. Someone out there killed Joseph Larkin for a reason. If you start sticking your nose in, or if whoever did this decides you're becoming too much of a nuisance, then they could very well come after you. And I happen to like both of you quite a bit."

He gave their arms a reassuring squeeze and smiled.

"And beyond that, I want you to know that I'm here for you. Don't ever hesitate to give me a call."

Maggie smiled. Maggie had never been as close to Jim as she had been to June, but she had always appreciated his candour and desire to help. He was smart and to the point. Even though Maggie was only his niece, he had always treated her as if she were his daughter. He had made a great cop in his prime, but no matter how busy he was, he had always made time for June and Kate. And whenever there was a problem, Jim would show up and help in whatever way he could.

So she knew his warning came from a place of genuine concern and affection.

"Don't worry," Maggie said. "We're being careful."

Biscuit wagged her tail excitedly as she shoved her snout against Jim's arm, demanding a pat.

"I'm sure you are," Jim said, smiling as he scratched Biscuit's head. He looked up and met Kate's eyes, and then Maggie's. "Just make sure you continue to be."

Chapter Sixteen

"I'LL SAY THIS ONCE, just for the record: this might not be the best idea," Maggie said as she and Kate drove towards the mansion. "Pretty sure I was warned last time that if I came back it would be considered trespassing."

"That's just Mr Lawrence flaunting his power," Kate said, dismissively. "He's harmless, really. What's the worst that could happen?"

"They'll call the police and have me arrested for trespassing?"

"If that happens," Kate said, "you can bribe the officers with biscuits. Seems to have worked so far."

"I tend not to bake just to avoid jail time. I'm far happier baking for myself," Maggie said, then added, "and Sweet Treats, I suppose."

"How's that going?" Kate asked. "Fine, as far as I can tell. Abigail hasn't told me anything about how they're doing or whether they're popular. Which probably means they're not selling and she's trying to protect my feelings."

"Or there just hasn't been time because people are clamouring for more," Kate said, rolling her eyes. "Or because she's a serial killer and has been too busy murdering tourists to keep tabs of how popular your biscuits are. Really, Maggie, you need some self-confidence. There's no reason for you to think that your baking isn't popular right now. Just give it time."

Maggie didn't say anything, though she tried to hold on to her cousin's encouraging words. They meant more than Maggie would ever admit, and she appreciated the casual, understated way Kate had said it, as if it were absurdly obvious.

"But this will be fun," Kate said, already onto an entirely different topic. "We'll wait around and see whether Mrs Larkin and Peter are up to something and then can go from there. We have to find out what's going on between them."

"We don't know the full story," Maggie said. "For all we know, I'm imagining things."

Kate shot her a look that so resembled June's that it was uncanny. "Do you really believe that?" she asked. "Honestly?"

"I'm just saying we shouldn't jump to conclusions," Maggie said. Though in all honesty, she was in perfect agreement with Kate. She didn't want to give her cousin the satisfaction of knowing that.

"Fifty pounds says I'm right," Kate said in a singsong voice. When Maggie went conveniently deaf right at that moment, Kate laughed.

When they reached the house, Maggie looked around. The sun was still rising overhead, casting early morning rays across the grounds. Birds chirped happily in the distance and the sea roared somewhere to the right beyond the edge of the cliffs. The entire place looked as though it could have been deserted, and it was slightly eerie.

"We're really early," Kate said, climbing out of the car and stretching. "The only people who will be here are the live-in staff like Chris and Mr Lawrence. I figure this is the best time to catch Peter and Mrs Larkin."

Maggie tilted her head and raised her eyebrows, a perfect imitation of Biscuit, who was currently lounging at The Book Nook. Considering what they were doing, inconspicuousness was a necessity, and as much as she adored the Cavapoo, she was only ever stealthy when she was stealing biscuits from under Maggie's nose.

"Assuming?" she asked. "I thought you were entirely convinced. Fifty pounds, right?"

"I am," Kate said. "But you seem to be in the mood for 'allegedly,' so I figured I'd humour you."

"You're so sweet," Maggie said. But another thought struck her. "Maybe it's not a great idea for me to be going in? As much as I want to find out what happened, Mr Lawrence has made it very clear that I'm not welcome. If he catches me..."

"You can't wimp out on me now!" Kate said. "We're already here." Her eyes got that puppy dog look to them as she begged.

Maggie sighed, chewing her lip and glancing around as she considered her options. Her eyes found the tin of biscuits and Kate's lunch, and an idea struck. "You go on ahead. I'll take your lunch. I wanted to talk to Chris about something. Assuming he's up. After that, I'll head out so Mr Lawrence doesn't catch me."

Kate's eyes brightened, and she nodded enthusiastically.

"Seems like a good plan," she said. "I'll let you talk to him alone. I don't think he likes me all that much."

"It's probably because you hate salad."

"That must be it."

She entered through the front door and crept through the halls towards the kitchen. Her ears were pricked for the sound of Mr

Lawrence's footsteps. She was going to have to do her best to hide from him.

But she got to the kitchen without incident. At first, she thought the kitchen was deserted. It was eerily silent, though the lights were all on, giving the room a cheery appearance that contradicted the oppressive silence that blanketed the room. Then a rustling sound came from a side room, and Chris strolled in, glancing down at his phone. He looked up, looked back down, before his head shot back up.

"What are you doing here?" he asked.

"Dropping off Kate's lunch," she said, holding up the Tupperware. "And biscuits. I was her ride this morning and she decided to make me her packhorse as well."

Chris gave a sympathetic laugh and moved towards the refrigerator, re-emerging a moment later with some eggs.

"I heard something interesting the other night," Maggie said casually.

"And what was that?" He grabbed a bowl and cracked an egg one-handed into it before picking up another.

"That your father," she said, "was Lowen Tredinnick."

The sound of his father's name caused him to botch the egg-cracking, sending tiny white shards into the bowl and yellow yolk running down his hand and onto the counter.

"What makes you say that?" he asked. He wiped his hand and tossed the napkin before grabbing three new eggs.

"Just a guess," she said. "Larkin managed to shut down his restaurant about ten years ago. That was your father, wasn't it?"

He didn't answer. Instead, he dumped the contents of the bowl and rinsed it, getting rid of the eggshell shards. But Maggie could see the tension that had taken over his body. Maggie waited, patiently, hoping that the silence that followed would elicit a response.

He calmly reached for a fresh bowl, and proceeded to crack eggs into it, one by one "Larkin decided he wanted the building. And it just so happened that Larkin came in one night and before we knew it, he had jumped up from his table, a look of wild-eyed fear on his face. From his throat came the most horrible, desperate sound of choking. But I find it difficult to feel any sympathy for him. Who would come into a restaurant and fake an anaphylactic reaction? Well, not faked, exactly. He really was having a reaction. There was no acting involved. When I later found out that it was an anaphylactic reaction caused by having eaten peanuts, I knew something was up. I knew for a fact there were no peanuts in his dish at all because I was the one who had made it for him. I was only eighteen, but I was already working full-time in the kitchen and that night I made all the starters that went out. In this business, we are well aware that not being vigilant of our customers' allergies is a matter of life and death, and the difference between success and ruin. He couldn't have even inadvertently eaten peanuts from his wife's dish because I ensured that neither of the starters that went out had any peanuts in them. I even made sure that there was nothing resembling a peanut remotely close to the workstation where I was cooking.

"I saw him choking and ran to the table just as Mrs Larkin was stabbing an EpiPen into his thigh. He seemed well enough to say he was going to sue for all we were worth as the ambulance came to take him away—he even went so far as to go to hospital. I went and checked his dish and found what I was sure was peanut residue. But he must have crushed up peanuts or something and hidden it in there. It was clear to me that this was a deliberate act of sabotage.

"And less than a week later we received a notice that he was suing my father," Chris said, taking a deep breath as he finished his story. "I had to testify as did everyone else. But he had better lawyers and they made it out that I was just a child who could so easily have made a mistake. They practically accused me of trying to kill him. In the fight for our livelihood, Dad lost everything, and he was never the same again. He just spiralled and he was no longer the person I once knew. Larkin had no idea of the devastating effect his actions had on me and my family."

"I'm so sorry," Maggie said, her voice filled with genuine sympathy. "I can't imagine how that must have felt."

Chris snorted, shaking his head. "When I got older, I managed to get a scholarship to go to culinary school. Then worked in a few kitchens up north. I kind of got into the habit of looking up Joseph Larkin to see what he was up to. I know, it's a weird form of torture. A couple of years ago, I saw they had a position for a cook. I figured if I got the job, I might be able to unearth some fresh information and clear my father's name."

"And neither of the Larkins recognised you from the trial? Surely your surname rang a bell?"

"Seriously?" he asked. "Do you think they cared enough to even remember the name Tredinnick or remember the face of some teenage cook they had seen in a trial years ago? It's clear they didn't care enough to even remember."

"So what now?" she asked. "Are you going to stick around? After everything that's happened?"

"My time is coming to an end here," he said. As he spoke he whisked the eggs effortlessly before pouring them into a pan. "There's no reason for me to stick around anymore. I'm already looking for new jobs. I'll stay here until I find one, and then I'm gone for good."

She hesitated. The obvious question was on her mind but she didn't quite have the courage to get it out. It was the kind of question that Kate would ask without thinking twice, but it wasn't so easy for her. For a moment she took inspiration from Kate, tapping into the kind of fearless spirit that she had, and it was enough for her to quickly get the question out.

"What were you doing the day Larkin died?" she asked.

Chris looked at her, his green eyes filled with irritation.

"Your detective friend asked me that already," Chris said. "Detective Pearce. He interrupted my surfing to ask me some pretty infuriating questions. And now you. But why don't you ask me what you really want to know?" Not even tapping into Kate's spirit was enough for her to get the question out, and the atmosphere was now so tense that she didn't know if she could take it any further. But it seemed as though she didn't have to. "No, I didn't," he said. "All I want is justice for my dad. I'm not murderous enough to kill for it. And if I was going to murder someone, there's no way I'd use Presidential Flour to do it. I don't know if you've ever thought about it, but there are plenty of other things in a kitchen that could kill someone without having to order it from the States. We have knives, ovens, chemicals. Even a frying pan could be a deadly weapon. Why on earth would anyone kill someone with flour? And besides, how would I have been able to afford it?"

He had a point, there.

Brushing past her, he headed towards the pantry.

"So is that why you keep coming by here?" he asked, crouching to rummage on the bottom shelf. "So you can ask me questions? He pulled out an onion. "Yeah, that's what I figured. If that's the case, I'd appreciate it if you left me well enough alone, all right? Now I need to get Mrs Larkin's breakfast ready and I don't like working in a messy kitchen."

"I'm sorry," she said, "it's just that—"

"Please..." he said, "I just want to do my work."

Maggie winced, feeling terrible about the whole thing and wanted to spend as little time as possible in this house. She didn't want to make any more enemies if she could help it.

She was about to slink out of the building when her phone buzzed. It was a text from Kate.

Up the stairs, to the right, and down the hall. Hurry!

Not wanting to stay another moment in the kitchen with Chris, she slipped into the rest of the house, running through the halls until she came to the grand staircase. She followed Kate's instructions and found her cousin crouched halfway down the hall behind a vase on a pillar.

"Anything?" Kate whispered when Maggie crouched next to her.

"I'll tell you later," Maggie whispered back. She was a little too shaken up to talk about it at that very moment. "What are we doing here?"

"Proving to you that I would've won those fifty pounds if you'd ended up making that bet."

The place seemed unnaturally still. In the early morning, it was far easier to believe that they were in Georgian times. The shadows were longer and the house felt more ancient. In the dim morning light, it was easy to admire Amélie Larkin's dedication to tradition and the old world. But even with it, the grandeur and the silence that permeated the house felt almost oppressive.

And then the silence was broken by giggles and soft voices. Kate and Maggie exchanged glances.

"Kate," Maggie whispered. "Where are we?"

"Not far from Mrs Larkin's bedroom," Kate whispered back, pointing to a door a little way down the hall.

Maggie's eyes widened at the implication. Whatever was going on, Mrs Larkin certainly wasn't alone.

Kate crept forward as if about to stick her ear to the door, and Maggie pulled her back by the arm. She jerked her head towards the end of the hall in silent communication. Kate gave her an exasperated expression, then followed her cousin.

"We need to find out if it is what we think it is," Kate said.

"We know what it is," Maggie rolled her eyes. "We don't need to corroborate."

Kate opened her mouth to answer, but before she could do so, the sound of a lock unlatching and the door opening interrupted her. Darting around the corner, the two of them peeked back along the corridor.

Peter sauntered out of the bedroom. His hair was messed up and his shirt was rumpled. As he stepped out, a slender hand with perfect nails and expensive bracelets dangling from the wrist reached out and turned him around. Maggie and Kate watched as Mrs Larkin kissed Peter passionately on the lips, before releasing him.

"Can you look at the Bentley today?" she asked casually as she straightened his shirt, her hands coming to rest on his broad shoulders. "It's making a strange noise and it's getting on my nerves."

"Of course," Peter said. "I'll get right on it."

"Thank you, darling."

Then without any ceremony, she turned and strolled back into her room as if nothing out of the ordinary had happened. The door closed and Peter began walking down the hall. His eyes landed on Maggie and Kate just as they were ducking back into hiding.

"You ladies aren't very good at sneaking around, are you?" Peter asked when he approached. He leaned against the wall as he observed them, a small smirk on his face and his arms folded.

"How long have you and Mrs Larkin been in a relationship?" she asked.

Peter snorted. "Relationship?" he asked. "It's nowhere near that serious. After Joseph, she has no interest in anything like that. And neither do I, for that matter."

"So it's an affair?"

He raised an eyebrow. "Her husband is dead," he said. "I don't think you can have an affair if neither of the parties are seeing anyone else. But, for a time, I suppose it would technically be considered an affair, sure."

"Why?"

Peter shrugged. "Does there need to be a reason? Amélie is gorgeous, and she was interested. And the gifts are definitely a perk."

"Gifts?" Kate asked. "What gifts?"

"Extra tips, use of the cars, nice clothes. Once she gave me a Cartier watch and told me to do whatever I wanted with it, including selling it. Couldn't believe it when I saw the price tag."

Then he turned his attention over to Maggie. "Though, for the record, that doesn't mean it's exclusive."

Maggie could feel herself going bright red. How was he this brazen after being caught with another woman?

"Did Joseph know?" she asked.

If he had gotten those kinds of perks, what would have happened if Larkin had found out about their affair or just about the gifts in general? If he had known how much his wife was giving to the handyman while he was in need of money, how would he have reacted?

But Peter shrugged again. "No idea. If he did, he didn't let on." At Maggie's dubious expression, he added, "If you think he might have, why don't you ask Chris?"

That was one of the last things she would have expected him to say. "Chris?" she asked.

"Yeah. I don't know him super well, to be entirely honest, but I saw him lurking around more than once. Considering he's obsessed with that kitchen, whenever I saw him outside of it, I always noticed. There was one time when I was working in the garden when I saw him wandering around, peeking into nearly every window. It was weird. Asked him about it and he gave me a vague excuse that I don't even remember."

That would make sense if he was trying to find dirt on Larkin, Maggie thought.

"Right. I've got to get going. There's a Bentley outside that needs some love and attention," Peter said, pushing himself away from the wall. He ran his fingers through his hair, making it look windswept and incredibly attractive. Then he looked Maggie directly in the eye again and smiled. "Think about what I said, love."

And he walked away without a second glance.

Kate turned to look at Maggie. "Did he really just flirt with you?" Maggie couldn't help feeling that Kate was a little astonished that it wasn't her who had been the recipient of his attention. Maggie didn't know whether to be flattered or not.

"I'm pretty sure he did," Maggie said. "Though how serious he was being, I don't know, and I don't have any interest in finding out."

Kate shrugged. "I mean, he's cute," she said. "And I know you don't want anything serious, so—"

"He just admitted to having an affair with Mrs Larkin, Kate," Maggie said, a little exasperated. "I'm not that desperate."

Maggie's stomach plummeted as she heard a slow, deep voice behind her.

"What are you two doing?"

Both women turned, and Maggie found herself staring at Mr Lawrence's ice-blue eyes.

"I was just dropping my cousin off," Maggie said. She knew it would not work this time.

"Your cousin is not a child. She does not need to be hand-held all the way into the house. You can just as easily drop her off at the gate," Mr Lawrence said, doing very little to hide his contempt for Maggie. "I believe, Miss Treloar, that I asked you to stop distracting your cousin at work and to stop coming into the house uninvited?"

Before Maggie could even think of a plausible excuse, it got worse. The door to Mrs Larkin's office opened, and footsteps came towards them.

"Mr Lawrence?" Mrs Larkin asked. "What's—?"

But then she rounded the corner and her eyes honed in on Maggie and Kate. Maggie could see the thoughts running through her head as she guessed what the two women had been doing there. Her eyes narrowed.

"What are you two doing here?" she asked.

"We were—" Kate said, and for the first time, she actually seemed a little nervous.

"Snooping," Amélie interjected, her voice full of venom. It was clear to Maggie that she was wondering how much they had seen or heard. "And I thought that Mr Lawrence asked your cousin to stop coming by all the time."

"I—"

"Mr Lawrence," Mrs Larkin said, interrupting yet again, "I would appreciate it if you called the police. It appears that we have two trespassers."

"But I work here."

"Not anymore," Mrs Larkin said, coldly through clenched teeth. The woman was livid. Her posture was rigid, her face a little reddened. Maggie sensed a fury that she was keeping bottled beneath the surface. "Get off my property. I'm reporting you to the police and if you ever come here again, I promise it will be the last thing you ever do."

Mr Lawrence escorted them through the house hurriedly and without any courtesy. When they stepped out into the morning sunshine, he slammed the door behind them.

"Well," Kate said, smoothing the front of her skirt. "That could have gone better."

~~~

They left the property without incident and drove down the cliffs back to town. At first, Maggie was worried that Mrs Larkin would follow through with her threat to call the authorities. She kept waiting for a phone call or a knock on the door from the police, but no one came, and she started breathing a bit easier.

Maggie was lounging at home watching TV when the doorbell rang. Biscuit woofed excitedly and bolted towards the door, her tail wagging enthusiastically. Maggie paused the show, stretched, and walked over to let Kate in.

But when she opened the door, she found herself looking at the unsmiling face of Detective Inspector Tom Pearce.

"Hi, Maggie," Tom said. For once there was no amusement in his eyes or any sign of familiarity. "Can we come in?"

Maggie glanced behind the man to see Matthew shifting back and forth uncomfortably, as if he didn't want to be doing this. Biscuit had run excitedly towards the constable as soon as the door opened and was jumping on him, trying to get his attention, her tail wagging and her tongue lolling to one side. When Matthew continued to ignore her, the Cavapoo sat on her haunches and whined softly, still looking up at him.

"Sure," she said, and stepped back.

There was a long uncomfortable moment in her living room as they all regarded one another. Maggie's stomach had twisted itself into an uncomfortable knot and tied itself tight.

Finally, Tom said, "I'm guessing you know why we're here, then."

"I can guess," Maggie said. She hugged her chest unconsciously. "I didn't think she'd actually do it."

"Well, she did," Tom said angrily. "And I'm having to take care of it."

"But we found out she was having an affair with Peter—"

"And if we'd found that out on our own, we might have been able to use that information," Tom snapped. Maggie took a step back at the anger in his voice. "As it is, it's your word against theirs, and they'll be able to remove all proof of it. So if it was relevant to the case, you could have really messed things up."

Maggie looked away.

"I'm sorry," she said. "I was just trying to help."

"I know you were." And though there was a softness in his tone, he did not manage to mask his frustration. "But that doesn't change the fact that you could have hampered an actual investigation, and you've seriously pissed off Amélie Larkin. She's onto you now."

"Are you going to arrest me?" she asked.

"No," Tom said. Maggie gave a relieved sigh and her body relaxed. "I managed to convince her not to press charges."

"Thank you."

"You can thank me by dropping whatever case it is you think you're investigating," Tom said, "and leave it to the professionals." And she finally realised just how angry he really was. It wasn't in his words or tone, but everything about him radiated disapproval. "You and your cousin. I've already talked to her, but I don't think she's going to listen. This has to stop. I've been indulging you two, and I can't keep doing it."

Maggie winced. She glanced over at Matthew, and she saw how uncomfortable he was. He was looking everywhere but at Maggie and Tom. For a moment, her curiosity stirred, and she considered asking him what was wrong. But the words dissolved in her mouth as she turned her attention back to Tom.

"I promise," she said. "But I swear they were having an affair. Peter admitted it, and he said she gave him gifts all the—"

"I'm sure he did," Tom said. "But whether we'll be able to prove that anymore remains to be seen."

"I... okay."

He sighed, his shoulders slumping as he ran his fingers through his hair. "I've got to get going," he said, deliberately avoiding eye contact with Maggie. "Take care of yourself. But if I catch you near this case again... just... make sure I don't, okay?"

The lump in Maggie's throat had turned to stone, and it was hard to swallow.

Tom nodded, and Matthew gave an awkward wave as the two of them left.

Maggie stayed in the entryway, the rock in her throat slowly shrinking even as the guilt and horror at what had happened began to surge.

The longer she thought about it, the more it sunk in, and the worse she felt.

She sighed and resigned herself to the sofa. Closing her eyes, she tried to gather her thoughts and push down the wave of embarrassment that was rising through her body.

A cold, wet nose pressed against her hand. Biscuit wriggled her head beneath Maggie's hand and when Maggie opened her eyes, she found her looking up at Maggie with concern.

"Thanks, Biscuit," Maggie said, scratching the dog behind the ears. "Come on, I think we both could use some comfort food."

Chapter Seventeen

KATE NEARLY BANGED DOWN Maggie's door the following morning.

"You're lucky I get up early," Maggie said, yawning. "Do you want some coffee?"

"Ooh, coffee sounds lovely," Kate said. "But we've got to get going. We don't want to miss it."

"Miss what?" Maggie's eyes narrowed suspiciously, and she folded her arms. "What are you not telling me?"

"So, I may have been texting Matthew, and he may have let slip that they're heading over to George Evans' house today," Kate said. "And seeing as I just got fired, I don't have anywhere better to go—"

"Wait, when did you get Matthew's number?"

"Hmm?" Kate asked, a little too innocently. "Oh, just some time. I may have wandered by the station a couple of days after we brought the biscuits."

"Kate—"

"Look, do you want to chastise me, or do you want to go over to George Evans' house?"

"I want to chastise you," Maggie said. She folded her arms, and she was actually frowning at her cousin, something that was a bit of a rarity. "Didn't Tom and Matthew come talk to you as well?" "Of course they did," Kate said, rolling her eyes. "They kept talking about how it was dangerous and that they were letting me off easily and that I should keep out of things."

"And you don't think you should listen to them?" Maggie asked.

"Of course not. It's not like they meant it."

"I'm pretty sure they did, Kate." Maggie was aware that her cousin didn't always listen, but she had expected that the threat of arrest would, at the very least make her reconsider or give her cause for concern.

"Stop being so negative," her cousin said. "We're so close, I can feel it. We can't give up now."

"We can, and we will," Maggie said. "Kate, you're not thinking about this clearly. You're upset that someone told you what to do and—"

"I am not," Kate said, perhaps a bit too defensively.

"Yes, you are."

"Are you going to help me or not?" Kate asked.

Sitting between them, Biscuit's head moved back and forth as the two women talked, following the exchange like one might a tennis match. Her head was cocked, one ear slightly pricked as she watched, her brown eyes looking worried and uncertain.

"No," Maggie said. "We have to put an end to this right now."

"Fine," Kate said, her voice biting, her anger rising. "Fine. It's not like I need any help." Kate stood up.

"Don't be like that, Kate, please…At least stay and have coffee. You can even have a biscuit with it." Kate looked at Maggie.

"No. I don't want any of your biscuits," she said, a little too harshly, and let herself out, shutting the door with a slam.

Maggie slumped on the sofa, and Biscuit instinctively moved closer to her. Nothing seemed to be going right at the moment and she seriously considered just getting straight back into bed. But she had work to do, and busying herself with something was going to distract her far more than lying in bed with the duvet over her head.

But as she started towards the kitchen, something started nagging at her. She thought about Kate and what her next move would be. She was clearly so determined to solve the case that she was going to jump in head first and Maggie could not help but feel that Kate was running out of luck. She could get in some serious trouble if she wasn't careful. And she foresaw what Kate was about to do, where she was heading at that very moment.

"Oh, no," Maggie said, and she ran to grab her car keys.

~~~

If the Larkin house was a monument to England centuries ago, George Evans' was a monument to cutting-edge architecture. It was sleek and minimalist, with organic curves and bare white walls. Dozens of floor-to-ceiling windows displayed jet black furniture and hardwood floors, priceless modern sculptures and baffling abstract paintings.

Usually, Maggie might have admired the stunning lawn or the expansive house. But she was too preoccupied and too consumed with anxiety to focus on anything else. All she could focus on was Kate's tiny red car tucked back away from the house, hidden from view unless you were looking for it. Maggie drove a little way further, parking off the property before hurriedly turning off the car and doubling back on foot.

If she could just get Kate away from the house before they were spotted, they could pretend the whole incident never occurred, and neither Tom nor anyone else would be any the wiser.

Maggie hurried past the front door, spotting Tom's car parked out front, and sprinted along the house, dodging the windows and ducking behind bushes to hide herself from view whenever possible. She had no idea how to find Kate. She couldn't call out, as that would defeat the purpose of a stealthy retreat. The abundance of large windows made it seem impossible that the occupants inside wouldn't notice her running across the grounds.

Mercifully, she saw the top of a blonde head of hair poking out from behind some bushes next to an open window. Indiscernible voices filtered from inside, but Maggie was more preoccupied with the crouching figure of Kate.

The bushes rustled traitorously as Maggie moved into them trying to reach her cousin. Kate's head spun around and her eyes lit up with excitement. But then the enthusiasm diminished when Maggie shook her head emphatically and tugged at Kate's arm, trying to get her to come with her. Kate yanked her hand away before bringing a finger to her mouth. Maggie opened her mouth to protest, but stopped herself when she registered the conversation happening a few feet from them. If she made any noise now, they were going to get caught.

Kate turned away from Maggie and went back to eavesdropping enthusiastically. Maggie forced herself not to give a very audible sigh of defeat. If Kate wasn't going to leave, the least Maggie could do was make sure her cousin didn't get into any trouble.

And as she resigned herself to the situation, she focused her attention on what was being said inside.

"Do you not have staff on hand?" Tom's voice filtered through the open window.

"I have a cleaning crew who comes twice a week and a gardener, but that's it," Evans said. "I don't see the need for anyone else. I'm perfectly capable of taking care of things myself."

If that was a casual jab at the Larkins, then it was a subtle one. There was no hint of judgment or disdain in his voice. But something told her that he thought less of the Larkins for keeping staff. Maybe it was because Larkin had owed him so much money but was still employing people.

Tom seemed to be thinking along the same lines, because he said, "You certainly live a very different lifestyle than your former partner."

"I really don't like using the term partner when it comes to Joseph," Evans said. There was a soft squeaking sound, as if he were reclining back in his chair. "As I've said before, the whole point of our arrangement was for me to be an angel investor of sorts. He wanted all the credit for the success and just needed financial support. I didn't mind staying in the shadows, so we came to an agreement. He made the decisions, and I kept out of it except for when it came to money. At the end of it, I'd get my money back plus a percentage of the profit. If it failed, I would still get my initial investment returned to me. It all seemed like a rather safe bet on my part, and I could afford it."

"That didn't seem to end particularly well for you," Tom said.

"No, it didn't."

Maggie peeked inside for the briefest of moments. George Evans was sitting on a leather office chair behind his sleek desk while Tom was sitting on the other side. He was leaning forward, engaged in the conversation, while Matthew hurriedly took notes next to him.

"The main issue I noticed after Larkin's death was that he had been dishonest about how willing people were to sell their properties. He led me to believe that several people, June Edwards and Sam Murphy included, were all waiting eagerly to sign. But when I reached out after his death, I found out that nothing could have been further from the truth."

"He lied to you?"

"That's an accurate summation, yes."

"How well did you know Mr Larkin?"

"I got to know him a few years back when he reached out to me about being an investor. Before that, his name had emerged in reference to a couple of lawsuits I had been made aware of and that was all."

"Did you ever get the impression, in your professional opinion, of any of these lawsuits being fraudulent?"

There was a long pause. Twigs dug into Maggie's knees where she crouched and her palms pressed against the soft soil. Something slimy brushed against her finger. She looked down to find a snail touching the side of her hand, contemplating whether it wanted to make the climb. She gasped and whipped her hand away.

"No," Evans said. "I had no idea. If I had, I wouldn't have helped him in the first place."

Tom remained silent, waiting for him to go on. The silence continued, smothering everything like a blanket. It started to get uncomfortable, then nearly intolerable. Maggie waited, suddenly afraid to breathe for fear of being heard.

Finally, George Evans broke the silence. There was another squeak as he shifted in his seat.

"If that's all, Inspector," Evans said, I should really get back to work. I appreciate all the hard work you have put into the investigation and I'm sure you have plenty to do—"

Evans fell quiet as if Tom had cut him off. "We're not quite done yet, Mr Evans," Tom said. "I have a couple more questions. The first of which is why are you lying?"

"What do you mean?" Evans asked.

"You knew about the lawsuits being fraudulent, didn't you?" Tom asked.

There was casual warmth and friendliness to Tom's voice, but it was wrapped around stony professionalism. He wasn't here to make friends; he was here for answers, regardless of how personable he seemed. It contradicted the man Maggie knew, yet it remained unmistakably him – the flip side of the coin, so to speak.

"I—"

"Mr Evans, one thing I can't stand is people lying to me," Tom said. "I've gotten fairly good at knowing when that's happening - like right now. I would much prefer it if you were honest with me. It would save us both a great deal of headaches later."

"I found out about it after the fact," he admitted. "I never had any confirmation of it. I only heard rumours. But they were enough to make me concerned. I tried to pull out of the arrangement but it proved more difficult than it should have."

"So Larkin lied to you and arguably scammed you out of thousands, if not millions, of pounds," Tom said. "That seems like an excellent motive for murder."

Evans snorted derisively. "Trust me, Inspector, I'd sue him before resorting to murder."

"If you sued him, you might not have gotten a penny," Tom pointed out. "His bank records show he didn't have nearly as much money as he claimed. He was practically bankrupt."

"If you're so suspicious of me," he said. "You should look at my travel records. I was in York at a business meeting that entire week. A dozen people can corroborate that."

Tom said, "We'll be sure to look into—"

Kate sneezed.

There was a long, terrible silence as the sneeze dissipated into the air. Maggie waited, hardly daring to breathe.

Footsteps sounded from inside. A moment later, Tom had appeared at the open window. His eyes swept the grounds before eventually landing on Maggie and Kate. His eyes narrowed.

"Anything the matter, Inspector?" Evans asked.

Tom looked behind him, before glancing back at Maggie. She watched him mouth *Car... Now...* before he turned back.

"Nothing that I could see. But I think we've gotten all that we need for the time being. We will be back in touch if we have any further questions."

Maggie turned to look at Kate. She no longer looked triumphant or excited. Maggie glared at her, before jerking her head in the direction that she had come and crawling backward from the bushes.

"I told you this would happen," Maggie hissed. "I warned you. But you wouldn't listen."

"It'll be fine," Kate said, but the anxiety in her blue eyes and the fact that her face was unnaturally pale made it clear she didn't believe it.

Tom was waiting next to the black sedan he always drove, talking in hushed whispers to Matthew. The inspector's eyes were hard as steel as he spoke. Matthew looked uncomfortable, looking down at the ground.

As they approached, they could pick up what Tom was saying.

"I mean, really, Matthew, what were you thinking?" Tom asked.

"I thought she was just curious," Matthew said, his voice panicked and slightly pleading. "I didn't think she was going to show up. I didn't think she would do something like that."

"No, Matthew, you weren't thinking," Tom said. "You're a police officer. You can't divulge important information relating to the case to everyone. I can't let you off with just a warning on this one."

"What are you going to do?" Matthew asked. Maggie could see the young man's eyes, his round face stricken and worried. "I'm sorry, sir, but—"

Tom glanced over and saw Maggie and Kate. He held up a hand and Matthew fell silent, shuffling a couple of feet back and staring down at the asphalt, looking anywhere but at Kate and Maggie.

"You two," Tom said, "are in a lot of trouble."

There was no friendliness or warmth in his voice, only the harsh cadence of a detective. Goosebumps raced up Maggie's arms as her stomach contracted painfully. She thought she might be sick.

"We were just—"

"Trespassing," Tom said, finishing Kate's sentence for her. "You were just trespassing. And I told both of you that if I caught you near this case again, there were going to be consequences. Do you remember that?"

"We're sorry, Tom," Maggie said, trying to mollify the situation.

"I don't want your apology," Tom said. "I want you both at the station. If you're not there in ten minutes, I'll find you and drag you there myself."

Chapter Eighteen

MAGGIE AND KATE WERE separated at the village police station. Maggie wound up in a small room, one with barely enough space for a table and three chairs. The glaring panel lighting above her head caused it to be excessively bright, and the bare walls, long-ago coated with an ugly off-white, seemed to be determined to close in on her. The chairs dug into Maggie's back and tilted one way or another on uneven legs every time she moved. She had thought the uncomfortable environment trick detectives were supposed to use was just something you found in TV shows, not in Sandy Cove. She guessed she had been wrong.

She looked at the clock on her phone yet again. Tom had left her there alone since he'd first closed the door almost an hour ago. At least he'd let her keep her mobile. Still, the entire situation just left her more time to ruminate on everything that had happened.

It was impossible for her not to be angry at Kate. This was all her fault, after all. Maggie had been content to leave everything alone after the incident at the Larkins' manor, but her cousin was stubborn, and prone to ignoring orders that inconvenienced her. The only reason Maggie was in trouble was because she had tried to keep Kate from getting into a hole she couldn't dig herself out of, which was exactly what happened.

She sighed and slumped forward, rubbing her face. That wasn't entirely true. Deep down she too had wanted to hear what Evans had to say. She might not have gone if she hadn't been trying to protect her cousin, but she should have forced Kate to come with her as soon as she had spotted her hiding in the bushes.

Everything was a mess, and all she wanted to do right now was be back home. She was exhausted and she would have given anything to be back on her sofa.

She even tried to lay her head down on the cold metal table in front of her, using her hand as a rather uncomfortable pillow, but was interrupted by the door popping open.

Tom looked into the room, his eyes still as hard as they had been back at Evans' mansion. She waited for the scolding, or for him to tell her he was arresting her. But instead, all he said was, "You can go."

Maggie stood, then came up short when she saw who was behind Tom in the hall. It was her Uncle Jim, unsmiling. Yet again, that feeling of being a teenager.

"Come on," Jim said.

She had just emerged when a door opened further down the hall and Kate flounced out, wearing a wide, confident smile that vanished the instant she saw her father's expression. Her normally tan features paled, and she seemed to shrink within herself.

"Outside. Now." As the two women passed, he said to the inspector, "Thanks for this, Tom."

"Yeah," Tom said. "But if I see them near this case again..."

"Don't worry," Jim said, "you won't."

It was only noon. The sun beat down overhead when they stepped out of the station, and the humidity clung to Maggie's skin.

"You two don't realise how lucky you are," Jim said. "Tom called me to tell me what happened, and I managed to convince him not to press charges. But he is a hard man to convince. You should have heard just how outraged he was."

"Thanks, Dad," Kate mumbled.

"What were you thinking?" Jim demanded, rounding on his daughter. "I have no doubt as to who came up with this scheme. I know you like to ignore the rules, but this is different. And Maggie, I would have thought you'd have more common sense than that."

"It wasn't her fault, Dad," Kate said. "She was coming to try and stop me."

"Then you should have listened to your cousin," Jim said. "Do you know Matthew's on probation now?"

Kate was horrified to hear that. "What?"

"He told you where they were going even though he knew Tom wanted you away from it all. He's lucky he didn't get fired."

"But that wasn't his fault, either," Kate said. Her eyes were wide with panic and guilt. "I convinced him to tell me."

"And he should have ignored you," Jim said. "Just as you two should have dropped it when the police told you. And you forgot to mention that Amélie called the police on you last time you were at the manor."

"But—"

"But nothing," Jim said. "I don't care how old you are, Kate Elizabeth Edwards. If you keep acting like a child then I'm going to treat you like one."

Kate bowed her head, nodding silently.

"And don't think you're getting off easily, Maggie," Jim said, turning to her. "I have half a mind to tell your parents what happened. If you were younger, I would. But really, I thought two women in their twenties would have more sense than this."

"I'm sorry, Dad," Kate said.

"Me too," Maggie added.

"I don't want sorry," Jim said. "I want change. And if this happens again, you're on your own. I'm not getting you out of it a second time. Now get to the shop. June wants a word with both of you."

Kate looked even more horrified than before. "Dad, you didn't—"

"Of course I did," Jim said. "She's my wife and your mother. Now get going before she has even more time to get her temper up."

~~~

Maggie didn't think waiting an hour or five minutes would have made a difference when it came to June's anger. By the time they arrived, she was already fuming.

"You two," June said the instant Jim ushered them into The Book Nook, "are absolutely mad. I didn't think it was possible for dyed hair to turn grey, but you two managed to make it happen. I swear you're going to be the death of me. And when were you going to tell us you lost your job?"

Normally, Kate might have protested, or said that her mum was overreacting. But this time, she just hung her head and nodded.

Maggie wanted to curl into a ball and pretend none of this had happened. Or, better yet, find a time machine and go back to this morning and prevent any of it from happening in the first place. But since time travel wasn't possible, she stood there and listened to June scolding her, feeling an ever-stronger sense of humiliation with every word.

Finally, the rant died away, though it didn't feel much like a reprieve. Maggie's face was burning hot and every sentence of June's rant was branded into her brain. She knew this was something she would replay over and over again in her mind for who knew how long.

"It won't happen again, Mum," Kate said, when June finally seemed to be finished. "I promise."

"I should certainly hope not," June said. "If I hear of anything like this again, I'll haul you to the station myself, do you understand? That goes for you, too, Maggie."

"Yes, Aunt June," Maggie said, nodding softly.

"Good. Now go shelve these books. And Kate, since you lost your job, I see no reason why you can't do a bit of cleaning with all that free time you will have now."

It was both of their least favourite jobs. But they still nodded and went about their tasks without complaint.

~~~

Later that day, as the sun dipped into the west-facing ocean, Maggie returned home, still reeling from her terrible day. Biscuit was eagerly waiting for her at the door, wagging her tail and bouncing with excitement, clearly thrilled to see her human.

"Sorry to have left you for so long, girl," Maggie said, scratching her Cavapoo behind the ears. "It's been a rough day."

Fortunately, Maggie had installed a pet flap in her back door for Biscuit's convenience. However, after the day's events, Maggie felt that her dog wasn't the only one who could use a long walk.

Despite her exhaustion, Maggie put on Biscuit's harness, grabbed the Cavapoo's lead, and took her outside. Though Biscuit had no idea what had happened, it was evident that she sensed something was wrong. She whimpered and nudged affectionately at Maggie's hand, looking up with adoring, soulful eyes that always seemed to know and understand more than a dog should.

They got back home, and Maggie curled up on the couch. She indulged in a mindless TV show, avoiding the need for any deep thought. Biscuit hopped up on the sofa and splayed out next to her. Maggie wrapped her arm around the dog like a body pillow, curling her fingers around the ruby-coloured fur and snuggling into Biscuit, getting a bit of comfort in the warmth radiating off her companion.

The show failed to lift her spirits. Her mind kept drifting back to the manor and the small interrogation room, to Uncle Jim's disappointed face and Aunt June's angry one. The guilt squirmed and gnawed at her.

Even as she watched the show, her eyes kept flicking back to her phone. There were no messages, not even from Kate, who was probably feeling just as miserable as Maggie was. But she wasn't looking for a message from her cousin. Though she didn't have Tom's number, she kept having some irrational hope that she would get a message from an unknown number, wanting to sort out what had happened earlier that day.

Maggie had never tried to explain things to Tom. While her intention might have been to protect Kate, the reality remained that she had been present, eavesdropping, and unable to control her cousin. She didn't wish to tell her side of the story as an attempt to justify her actions, as it didn't feel right to throw Kate under the bus. However, she still wanted to speak to Tom, seeking some assurance that things would eventually be okay.

But her mobile remained dark and silent the entire evening until she fell asleep on the couch, the TV still on.

Chapter Nineteen

THE FOLLOWING SAY, MAGGIE remained at home, curled up on the couch. It was her day off, and despite her usual habit of stopping by The Book Nook, she didn't want to confront her aunt or the rest of the MBC right now.

Helena and Liv had texted her, neither of them scolding her, but she could tell just by their tone that they were getting their information from June and neither seemed particularly happy with her. Liv was undoubtedly worried that Maggie and Kate had jeopardised Sam's case. Helena was friendly enough, but her text referenced bad energy and an offer of a Reiki session after her yoga class ended, which was a blatant comment that the older woman thought Maggie was out of line and needed some help. The offer was one that Maggie had accepted in the past, but this time she didn't respond.

The only text that made her smile a little was the one from Bert that came in around noon. All it said was: *Welcome to the delinquent club*. Then, a minute later: *Got arrested three times when I was your age. Don't worry too much about it.*

It was a strange sort of comfort, but again she didn't have the energy to respond.

At one point, she forced herself off the couch and turned the oven on, planning to bake shortbread for herself and Biscuit, something that usually cheered her up. But by the time she had pulled out the butter and the oven dinged, she realised that she didn't have the motivation.

What was worse was that her mind kept creeping back to the case, no matter how hard she tried to prevent it from doing so. She couldn't help but think that even though she had the information she needed, she was still one step behind where she should have been.

If only she could piece it all together...

No. She was done. She wasn't going to keep doing this. She couldn't keep doing this.

She wrapped herself up in her blanket and turned the next episode of the trashy show back on.

When she went into The Book Nook the next day, June was still frosty. Kate was in the shop, too, sweeping and keeping her head down. It was fairly obvious that June had strong-armed her daughter into working at the shop as a form of penance. June nodded at Maggie as she walked to the counter. The biscuit jars were nearly empty.

Forcing herself not to sigh, she went into the back to work on inventory without June asking, and she stayed hidden in the office the entire day.

~~~

The next few days played out in the very same way, with Maggie and Kate both keeping their heads down as they worked at the shop. June was still cool towards the women, but warmed slightly every day as the girls continued to work hard and keep out of trouble.

The Friday after the chaos had hit, Maggie walked into The Book Nook to find June in a far better mood than she had been.

"You're just in time, Maggie," June said, turning away from the conversation she'd been having with another woman at the edge of the counter. It was the most June had said to her in a few days, and she was far friendlier than she had been since things had blown up. "You have a visitor."

Maggie was surprised to see Abigail standing at the counter. She looked to be in a very good mood, beaming.

"Maggie!" Abigail said. "It's so good to see you."

"Is this about the baking?" Maggie asked. "Did I mess something up? Was there something wrong with the biscuits?" Panic gripped her insides. What if she had undercooked something and made someone sick? Or what if she had messed up the recipe and everyone thought it was awful? After everything that had happened, more bad news about her baking was the last thing she needed. She didn't think she would be able to handle it.

She braced for the worst.

But Abigail was staring at her as if she had spoken in German. "What? No. Of course not. Actually, I came to give you this."

Abigail held out an envelope. Bemused, Maggie took it and sliced it open. It was a cheque made out to her for the biscuits she had baked for Sweet Treats. She looked at the sum, then looked at the sum again, certain she had misread it.

"I think you added an extra zero here," she said.

Abigail laughed and shook her head. "Not at all," she said. "Business picked back up this month, and your biscuits have been selling out. They're incredibly popular. I knew I should have sought out your expertise ages ago."

"That's fantastic," Maggie said. "I'm so glad things are looking up again."

Abigail nodded, smiling excitedly. "Do you think there's a chance you can do more? I know you're already making loads, but I would love it if we could work together more closely. You could even use the kitchen in the bakery to work on larger batches if you like. Then you won't have to carry them everywhere."

Maggie felt almost giddy. Her brain had turned fuzzy as she clutched the cheque in her hand. She was so stunned by the turn of events that it barely registered that Abigail was continuing to speak.

"Sorry, what was that?" Maggie asked.

"I was wondering if there were any other biscuits you could make," Abigail said. "I'm happy to shake up our collection if there's something you think you could nail."

"Oh, that's easy," Kate said. "Her shortbread. It's the best. So authentic."

Biscuit's head popped up at the word 'shortbread', eyes darting from person to person as her tail thumped hopefully. When no one produced her favourite treat, she whined softly.

"I remember you brought them last time, but I didn't try any. If you bring them by the shop, I'd be happy to do a side-by-side comparison to mine," Abigail said. She pulled out her phone and checked the time. "I've got to get going. I need to prepare some sourdough to bake for tomorrow. But come by in the next couple of days and we'll iron out the terms of the deal."

"Yeah, of course. I'd love to." The words sounded more like squeaks than anything coherent, thought Maggie. "Thank you."

Abigail gave a warm smile as she walked purposefully towards the door. "I'll see you soon, then."

Kate at least waited until Abigail was entirely gone before giving a loud, piercing shriek that all but burst Maggie's eardrums and hugged her cousin.

"That's so amazing, Maggie!" Kate said, squeezing tight. Maggie made joking choking sounds as Kate attempted to suffocate her with a bear hug. "I told you how good your biscuits were. I'm so happy for you."

"It's just me baking biscuits," Maggie said modestly. "It's not that big of a deal."

"You're baking biscuits and getting paid for it," Kate said, finally releasing her. "Hasn't that been your dream for years?"

It was the most animated and most herself Kate had seemed since the police station. There was nothing but unadulterated pride and excitement on the woman's face, but it was heat that rose up through Maggie's face. The truth was that, yes, she had always thought baking professionally would be fun, but she had never actually thought it would happen. She had known she was good at baking, but she had never dared to do anything more than bake for friends and family.

"It's not much," Maggie tried to say.

"You need to start giving yourself more credit," June said, and she was smiling—for the first time in a week. And she sounded genuinely pleased and Maggie could imagine what Aunt June was thinking: that this was a fantastic distraction after everything that had happened. If anything could get her mind off the case and out of this funk, it was this.

Maggie was grinning just as broadly. After everything that had happened, it felt good to experience something positive for a change. Her knees were slightly wobbly as she glanced back down at the cheque.

Later that afternoon, as the delighted stupor wore off while she stocked shelves, part of her mind drifted away, back to a different partnership that hadn't ended as amicably.

When had George Evans figured out about Larkin's deception, precisely? In the interview, he'd sidestepped that little detail rather nimbly. Depending on when he'd found out, he could have been furious and wanted to exact revenge. He would have had enough money to not think twice about ordering something as absurdly expensive as Presidential Flour.

But that couldn't have happened. He'd been out of town. What about Peter? She had looked up the price of a Cartier watch, and the sum was more than enough for Peter to afford the flour. Chris was a possibility; he had a motive, but no funds.

No. She shook her head to clear the thoughts. She wasn't going down that route. She was done with that. And now she had something new to think about, something far more exciting. At least, that was what she told herself.

Chapter Twenty

"YOU SHOULD ADD SOME orange zest," Helena said, biting into a still-warm piece of shortbread.

"Pretty sure that defeats the purpose of a plain shortbread biscuit," Jim said, leaning against the wall as he bit into his own biscuit.

"But everything tastes better with orange in it!" Helena said. "Everyone knows that."

"Not everyone has the same obsession with orange as you do, Helena," Bert said.

"But shortbread doesn't taste any good without any orange in it," said Helena, sniffing derisively.

"At some point, I'll make some orange shortbread just for you," Maggie said. "But for now, I'm going to stick with the basics."

"Well done, love" Bert said, holding up a cup of tea. "Don't cave into Helena's peer pressure. Just stick to perfection."

The MBC were all crammed into the living room. Plates of biscuits were on a spread along the coffee table, everything from fairings to shortbreads to brandy snaps.

I never worked out what Tom's favourite biscuit was, Maggie thought. The uncomfortable sensation in her stomach made her push the thoughts away. She didn't want to think about Tom right now.

The reason she had been going crazy with baking all day was because she was test baking a variety of biscuits for Abigail. She was meeting with her in a few days to solidify their business arrangement, and she wanted to provide a decent selection for Abigail to pick from. As a result, Maggie's entire home smelled even more like biscuits than usual, and she still had many more delights to bake.

The oven dinged and Maggie hurried back to the kitchen to pull out another tray of brandy snaps. She grabbed a dowel and hurriedly curled the thin, lacy amber biscuits around the wooden rod before they cooled. She hissed at the heat but kept going until each one was wrapped around the dowel. Biscuit was sitting next to her, the dog's soulful eyes staring longingly at the biscuits that were so tantalisingly close.

"How's the restaurant going, Sam?" Maggie heard Kate ask in the living room.

"A bit better," Sam said as Maggie walked back in. "Still not back to what it was, but we're on an upward trend, so I think things are going to get better. After Larkin…" Sam trailed off, glancing nervously at June and Jim before looking at Kate and Maggie. Maggie understood. Ever since she and Kate had ended up in the police station, all of the MBC had been hesitant to bring up anything tangentially related to the murder. Based on June's brief glare in Sam's direction, she couldn't blame them.

"How have people been liking the latest book?" June asked, trying to change the subject. "It hasn't been my favourite. It's not terrible, but I'm pretty sure I've got the killer figured out already."

"The butler?" Liv asked.

"I'm not saying," June said. "I don't want to spoil it for the people who haven't started reading yet."

She stared pointedly at Sam.

"I've read fifty pages so far!" Sam said. "And I've got an entire week."

"It's 450 pages."

Maggie smiled and turned away, going back to the kitchen now that the snaps had cooled a bit, but her brain had already gone unbidden into the dangerous territory that was the murder of Joseph Larkin. She fished around in her mind to try and come up with something else to think about. But it did no good. And the truth was that, no matter how hard she tried to deny it, she was still thinking hard about the case. It was an unwelcome daily occurrence. But it wouldn't leave her head. She knew there was something, she was missing. She just couldn't figure out what it was.

She began transferring the brandy snaps from the dowel to a tray, trying and failing to avoid thinking about the case. But then something clicked into place. She gasped and dropped the rod. It fell to the ground and the delicate biscuits shattered into a million pieces. Biscuit's tail began wagging furiously as she shoved her head down to the ground and began hoovering up the shattered pieces.

"Maggie?" June asked, poking her head into the kitchen. "Are you all right?"

She didn't answer, her mind was going a mile a minute as things began falling into place. It all made sense. She pulled out her phone, glancing at the clock. 5.30 pm. She might have enough time.

"I've got to go," Maggie said, and moved towards the front door. "Biscuit, stay here."

"But it's your house," Bert yelled after her. She didn't answer; she just darted out the door as fast as she could.

The lights in the police station were still on. Just as she arrived, a familiar figure was stepping out. Tom glanced over at Maggie.

"Maggie?" he asked. His voice was stiff, but it was still clear he was surprised to see her.

"I know you're still mad at me," Maggie said in a hurry. "And you have every right to be. But I had to come see you."

He sighed. His eyes were cool but he could not find it in himself to look at her. He looked as though he were considering walking away.

"Please," she said.

"Is it about the case?" She didn't miss the terseness in the tone, but she couldn't let that stop her. She had to tell him what she'd figured out.

"It is," she said.

Maggie could see the very frustration that he displayed the other day causing him to tense up. "Maggie..." he said. "I'm not going to tell you again—"

"I have an idea," she said, cutting him off. "I think I figured out what happened."

Tom hesitated, glancing back over his shoulder at the police station. Maggie's heart thundered in her chest. For a moment, she wasn't sure if he was going to talk to her at all. If he told her to leave, then she would. But she found enough courage to hold her ground.

But then Tom sighed and looked back at her, his brown eyes focused and intense.

"Well, then," he said. "I suppose we should go back inside."

A wave of relief surged over Maggie. A shaky breath she hadn't realised she'd been holding escaped her. She really didn't think he was going to listen to her.

"Thanks," she said.

Tom didn't say anything. He held the door open and gestured for Maggie to go in first.

The police station was nearly entirely empty. Two night shift officers were at their desks, looking at their phones. The one who had his feet up on the desk quickly pulled them off the moment he saw Tom. They both straightened up a little and hid their phones.

"Forget something, Inspector?" the man asked. His eyes found Maggie and watched her curiously. She could feel her face starting to flush. There was no way the officer didn't know who she was and how she had been brought in the other day.

"Something like that," Tom said. "We'll be out of your hair in a few minutes."

"No worries," the officer said. "It's a slow night, anyway."

"Like every night," said the other officer, laughing.

Tom didn't react and just continued on to his office.

Once he had closed the door, he turned to her and said, "Okay, so tell me." He sounded sceptical, but Maggie knew she had to speak with confidence. She had to do everything she could to make him believe her.

Maggie started to tell him what she had figured out.

Tom listened, leaning against the wall with his arms folded. His eyes locked onto her, unmoving as she started her theory. She felt as though they were boring into her, dissecting her. His face was unreadable as he listened intently. It was so inscrutable that she wasn't even sure if he believed her, and worry and unease gripped her insides. When she finally finished, she waited, holding her breath as she waited for his verdict.

"Can you confirm it?" he asked. "Do you have actual proof or is this all just guesswork?"

"It's all just guesswork, I suppose," Maggie admitted, a little reluctantly. "But I am certain I've figured it out and I knew I had to come and tell you immediately."

"Well, I'm glad you're still not taking matters into your own hands."

There was a long, uncomfortable pause as Maggie thought back on their last interaction. There were a dozen things she wanted to say to Tom, and they all swirled back and forth in her head, and it was nearly impossible for her to pick out what to say first. Eventually, though, her brain settled on something.

"Is Matthew all right?" she asked.

"He will be," Tom said. "He's a good kid, just a little easily distracted. Especially by Kate."

"She has that effect on people, when she wants to," Maggie said. "Is he still in trouble?"

"Yes."

"It wasn't his fault," she said.

"He should have known better," Tom said. "And he agrees with me. I think he'll be less easily swayed by biscuits and cute dogs and pretty girls in the future. He's got a lot to learn, but he's trying, and that's all I can ask for."

"I'm sorry," Maggie said softly. "I wasn't trying to eavesdrop. I was trying to stop Kate. It isn't an excuse, but that's what happened."

"I know," Tom said. "Kate came by and told me so yesterday. She wanted to apologise."

Maggie blinked. "Really?"

Tom nodded. "I think she wanted to patch things up, especially to get Matthew out of trouble. I don't think she expected that to happen to him."

"No," Maggie said. "I'm glad she did, though."

"Me too," he said. "Don't get me wrong. I'm still annoyed with the both of you. But I at least understand things a bit better now."

"It won't happen again," Maggie said. "I promise."

"I'll have to take your word on that. I'm guessing she doesn't know, then? What you just told me?"

Maggie shook her head. "Just you."

Tom nodded, looking back down at the ground in contemplation. His finger tapped against his bicep. Finally, he let out a deep exhalation and pushed himself off the wall, running his fingers through his hair.

"I'll look into it," he said. "If I can find it, then I think you're right. Otherwise, there's no way your theory works."

"I know. How long do you think it will take you to find it?"

He scratched the back of his head in thought, trying to run the numbers in his head. Finally, he said, "If I'm lucky, we'll both know by the end of tomorrow if your theory adds up."

"And do you think that it adds up?" Maggie asked tentatively. She was surprised at how nervous she felt, and even more surprised at how desperately she wanted to know if Tom agreed with her.

"You might be right," he said. "But I've learned you can't just jump on the first solution that makes sense, either."

"You mean like when you hauled Sam in for questioning," Maggie asked.

Tom eyed her, half-annoyed, half-amused. "Like that, yeah," he said. "I was wrong on that one, even if he was the most logical suspect. But that's how it goes sometimes. You know that."

"I do," Maggie said. "Trust me. Considering what Kate and I put you through, I don't think I can berate you for thinking it was Sam."

"Fair enough, we've both been idiots."

Maggie laughed. The tension that had been thrumming between them since he had seen her outside the station had finally begun to dissipate, and she was beginning to relax a little.

Then, before she even realised what she was doing, she blurted out, "If I'm right, can I come with you when you confront them?"

Tom frowned, his face suddenly shifting back to stern caution. "If I say no, are you going to show up anyway?" he asked.

"No," Maggie said, and meant it. "And I won't tell Kate, either. It'll just be me. Assuming you're okay with it."

Tom studied her, and she forced herself not to squirm under his gaze. Finally, he said. "I believe you." He sighed and ran his fingers through his hair. "All right, you can come. I'll let you know when it happens."

"Really?"

"As long as you listen to me and don't do anything stupid." He gave a small grin, and Maggie realised that, if he hadn't believed her assurances, he would have said no.

"I promise," she said.

They stood in silence, both waiting for the other one to say something.

Maggie was the one to break it. "I should probably get home," she said. "I kind of left all of the MBC at my house, and they've probably wondered where I've got to."

Tom nodded, pushing himself off the wall and back towards the door. "I'll see you out, then."

They walked out in silence, stepping into the warm, slightly muggy summer evening. The stars glittered overhead. After a long moment, Maggie said, "Thanks."

"For what?"

"For not telling me to leave when you saw me."

"There was never any danger of that," Tom said.

"In that case, for not arresting me when you caught me trespassing."

"That was all your uncle's doing," Tom said. "I was fully intending to process both you and Kate until he showed up and convinced me otherwise. I owed him a favour, so I let it drop."

Maggie thought about asking what that favour was, but decided against it. She had pressed her luck enough already, and if Tom or Jim wanted to tell her what that favour was, then they would. Until then, she would let it be.

"Thank you anyway," she said.

"It's fine." Tom pushed his hair out of his eyes and stared upward. "I'll let you know when I find something out."

Chapter Twenty-One

☆

MAGGIE WAS BREWING TEA when her mobile buzzed. Glancing down, she beamed when she saw a text from a number she had put into her contacts two nights prior. She opened it hurriedly, so excited that it took her a moment to unlock her phone.

Just got word. You were right. Heading to Larkin's at noon if you're still interested.

Grinning like a maniac, tea completely forgotten, she texted Tom back almost instantly. *See you there.*

She put her phone down and glanced over at Biscuit, who was eyeing the plate of homemade wagon wheels on the counter.

"No chocolate for you," Maggie said, tugging gently at the dog's collar. "Come on, let's finish getting ready. We've got a killer to catch."

~~~

It didn't occur to Maggie until later that, if she hadn't met Tom and Matthew at the gate, she probably wouldn't have been let in at all. So it was by a miracle that she ended up directly behind the now-familiar black sedan as they drove up the winding road to the Larkin's manor. They stopped at the ornate gate, which slowly opened a few moments after they pulled up.

Matthew and Tom clambered out of their car almost as soon as it stopped in front of the mansion. Matthew looked nervous as he regarded Maggie, but brightened significantly when Biscuit hurried out of the car, bolting directly for the constable. A boyish grin spread across Matthew's face, but he still glanced over at Tom before bending down and beginning to pet her.

"Hey girl, long time no see," Matthew said, then laughed as Biscuit eagerly lapped at his face, her tail and butt wiggling ecstatically. "Sorry I was so mean to you last time."

Biscuit, who had clearly forgiven Matthew for his shocking error of ignoring her the last time they had seen one another, gave a soft, happy *woof* before resuming licking.

"Doing all right?" Maggie asked Matthew.

"Better than I was," he said.

"Sorry about everything that happened," she said. "Kate and I didn't want you to get in trouble."

"It'll be okay," Matthew said. "And I think I can forgive you as long as you keep up with the regular biscuit deliveries."

"I'll see what I can do," Maggie said, smiling.

"Right," Tom said, taking a deep breath as he looked up at the house. "Let's get this over with, shall we?"

The door was already opening. A cold and annoyed-looking Mr Lawrence peered out imperiously, then his expression froze as he saw Maggie standing there next to Tom.

"Miss Treloar," Mr Lawrence said. "I believe I informed you last time that you are not welcome here."

Tom cleared his throat. "Miss Treloar is here as a personal favour to me," he said. "My constable hurt his wrist and is unable to take notes, didn't you, constable?"

"Huh?" Matthew looked up, blinking momentarily before he realised what was happening. "Oh, yes sir. It's still hurting."

Tom nodded before looking back at Mr Lawrence. "I understand if this is inconvenient to you and Mrs Larkin, but I assure you it's a necessity."

Mr Lawrence's eyes narrowed, and he looked as though he was going to argue. But he seemed to think better of it. Sighing, he held the door open further and let them inside.

"I trust this is important?" The steward sounded almost bored.

"Very," Tom said. "I would very much like it if I could speak to the entire household."

Lawrence gave a bitter smile. "I'm afraid that Mrs Larkin is in an important meeting right now and can't be disturbed."

"I dare say she and Mr Evans can take a few minutes break from their conversation," Tom said.

For once, Mr Lawrence looked unsettled, as though he hadn't expected Tom to know that Mrs Larkin was with Evans. Granted, it wasn't hard to surmise when you knew that the luxurious but practical car currently in the Larkin's drive belonged to George Evans.

Tom continued, seemingly oblivious to the other man's discomfort. "In fact, it's rather fortuitous. I think Mr Evans could be of great help in this meeting as well."

"If you're certain," Mr Lawrence said, albeit very reluctantly.

"I am."

"In that case, I'll take you to the parlour and bring everyone there."

An actual parlour room scene, Maggie thought, unable to hide her smile. *Helena and Kate are going to kill me for not including them.*

The parlour was a large room with stunning wood-panelled walls and lush, expensive furniture built to look as though they were from the Georgian era but Maggie concluded that they were almost certainly custom-made, and at great expense. Sun streamed through large windows, and Maggie had to wonder just how often this room was actually used, or if it had ever been used at all.

As she arched her head back to look up at the tall ceiling, the doors opened again, and Amélie Larkin stormed in, closely followed by George Evans. Behind them were two men in suits, one large and jovial looking, the other slightly trimmer and more stoic. Mrs Larkin was fuming, her eyes on fire, all of her anger trained on Tom.

"DI Pearce," Mrs Larkin said. "I believe I told you I wouldn't speak to you again unless my lawyer was present."

"And it appears as though he is," Tom said conversationally. "I'm not surprised, considering you and Mr Evans had a meeting today to iron out the financial issues between him and your late husband."

Mrs Larkin opened and closed her mouth, looking shocked. "And how did you know that?" she demanded.

"Mr Evans' assistant informed me he was here today," Tom said. "There's only one reason he would be here that I can guess. Which one of you is Mrs Larkin's lawyer?" Tom directed this last comment at the two other men.

"I am sir," the grim-looking one said. "And I would request that you—"

"Relax," Tom said, holding up a hand. "I'm not here for your client. Though I think she might want to stay for what's about to happen."

The lawyer suddenly looked far less grim and more at ease. He nodded at Tom in conciliation. Mrs Larkin, however, didn't appear to be finished.

"And what's *she* doing here?" she asked, pointing at Maggie, her blazing eyes narrowing to slits. "I told her she was no longer permitted on the premises."

"She's here in a professional capacity, Mrs Larkin," Tom said soothingly.

The door opened again, and Chris, Peter, and Lizzie walked in. Mr Lawrence walked in immediately behind them and closed the door.

"What's this about?" Mrs Larkin asked.

"I thought you would want to know who killed your husband," Tom said mildly.

"What?" Mrs Larkin rounded on the rest of the group, her eyes flicking to every person there. They all looked as shocked as she did. "Who?"

Tom raised his eyebrows. "Who had the most to gain?" he asked. "Really, I should have seen it ages ago. But everything fits neatly now that a couple of new pieces of information have come to light."

Mrs Larkin scowled, folding her arms as she glared daggers at the inspector. "Are you going to tell us, or are you going to prattle on?" she demanded.

"Very well," Tom said, nodding. "Mr Evans."

There was a long unpleasant pause. Then Evans laughed.

"You have to be joking, Detective Inspector," Evans said.

"You're one of the few people in this room who could afford Presidential Flour," Tom said. "In fact, I believe one of your keto-friendly restaurants up near York used to use it."

"I own the restaurants, I don't keep track of their inventory," Evans said tersely. Behind him, the jovial-looking man who had to be Evans' lawyer looked far less jovial. "Besides, you checked my travel records. I was nowhere near Cornwall when he died."

"True," Tom admitted. "The part about being in Cornwall, at least. Which is why you had someone else do the dirty work for you, someone who was just as interested in revenge as you."

"I told you that I didn't care about Larkin stealing my money."

"You cared that he conned you," Tom said. "Anyone would, and when you found out he'd conned others, you tried to get out of the deal. You demanded your money back and he refused. You might not have needed the money, but something like that would have damaged your business and reputation if your association with Larkin ever were to get out. Did he threaten to reveal it?"

"I never—"

"George," the lawyer said. "I think it might be best if you stopped talking."

"These are all insinuations," Evans said, waving his hands wildly. "I don't have to stand here and take this."

"You do," Tom said, most of the friendliness gone from his voice. "Or I'll take you down to the station and we can do it there. Your lawyer can come along with you."

"Enlighten me then," Evans said, nearly laughing. "How did I manage to be in two places at once?"

"You couldn't," Tom said. "But you supplied the murder weapon. Didn't he, Chris?"

Chris took a step backward, eyes darting between Tom, Evans, and the door. "What are you talking about?" he asked.

"You joined the Larkin household two years ago, didn't you?"

"Something like that," Chris said uneasily.

"Where did you work before then?"

"Up north."

"Could you be more specific, please?" Tom said, then looked down at his notepad. "Or, if you've forgotten, I can jog your memory. You were employed at a place called The Hopewood Inn, a rather luxurious restaurant near York. One that Mr Evans happens to own."

Chris hesitated. "Yeah, that was one of the places. But I never met Mr Evans."

"Are you sure about that?" Tom asked. "Seems a bit strange for a chef not to have at least met the owner. How did you find out about his and Joseph Larkin's partnership?"

"I didn't— I don't know what you're talking about," Chris said. His fingers were fidgeting nervously at his side, and he refused to meet Tom's stare.

"Miss Treloar made the connection," Tom said. "Or at least guessed at it. I followed up on your past employment, and there it was. So I'll ask you again, how did you find out about the partnership?"

Everyone was staring at Chris now. Lizzie's mouth was open. Peter's usual smug demeanour had been replaced by shock. Even Mr Lawrence looked surprised.

Still, Chris didn't say anything. Over in the corner, Evans was exchanging rapid whispers with his lawyer, looking more and more panicked.

"You don't have to answer," Tom said. "But I'd appreciate it if you did. Otherwise, I'll have to take both you and Mr Evans down to the station."

Chris eyed him. "You'll do that anyway if I confess," he said.

"True," Tom admitted. "But things will be easier for you if you talk."

"You don't have to say a word, Chris," Evans said. "I'll pay for you to have a lawyer."

"I saw you that day surfing," Tom said. "You left a little before I did. Were you waiting for Sam to leave and go back to his restaurant? I'm sure you knew that was where Larkin was going to wind up that day. Was he planning to do the same thing to Sam that he did to your father?"

Amélie Larkin's eyes shot open and she finally looked at Chris properly. "You're Tredinnick's son?" she asked. "I didn't..."

"Of course you didn't," Chris said, finally snapping. "You and your husband never even gave my family another thought." He rounded on Tom. "But that doesn't mean I killed him."

"Was he talking about running Sam out of business by making himself have an allergic reaction?" Tom asked patiently.

"Yeah, he was," Chris said. "He wasn't sure if he was going to, but he'd talked about it. Not when he went that day. He was just planning on badmouthing the place a bit. He wanted to see if he could go about it differently, getting the place shut down, I mean... He didn't want to raise suspicion by doing the same thing over again."

"How do you know all this?" Amélie Larkin's face was pale and mortified. Her lawyer had resumed his grim look and was hurrying to talk in Mrs Larkin's ear.

"And so when you found out he was going to the fish and chips restaurant, you figured you might as well help him out with that?" Tom asked.

"I told you," Chris protested. "I didn't kill him."

Tom nodded speculatively as he considered Chris. "And what if I told you we found fingerprints on the flour?"

Maggie nearly dropped her pen. Her head whipped around to look at Tom, her mouth open. There had been fingerprints? Why hadn't he told her? But as she looked at him, she caught the look in his eyes, that steely, calculating look. He was bluffing.

Chris' eyes were wide with alarm. "That's impossible," he said.

"Why would it be impossible?" Tom asked, almost casually, like he was chatting with an old friend.

"Because—" But Chris seemed to realise he misstepped. His face paled and his mouth clamped shut. His eyes darted toward Evans, and then back to Tom.

"Would you be willing to provide your fingerprints to eliminate you as a suspect?" Tom asked. Again, Chris said nothing. His hands flew into his pockets, as if trying to hide his fingertips.

"It's over, Chris," Tom said to the deathly quiet room. "I know it was you. Why don't you tell me what happened? How did you get the flour?"

All eyes were on Chris. He hesitated, but then his shoulders slumped, defeated.

He'd given me the flour ages ago," Chris said, nodding over to Evans. "Just told me to wait for a good opportunity while he was out of town. Everything lined up."

"Chris, stop talking," Evans snapped.

"How did you find out about one another's relationship to the Larkins?" Tom asked, before Chris could respond.

"It was just luck," Chris said. Now that he'd started, he didn't seem able to stop. "I didn't even know Evans was from Cornwall. But a couple of years ago, I saw them talking at one of the parties Mr Evans held at Hopewood. I recognised him immediately. When I got the chance later, I told Mr Evans what Larkin had done, and that he was bad news. He seemed pretty surprised, but thanked me and then left. I thought that was the end of it.

"Then, a few weeks later, he comes back to me. He asks me how badly I want to get revenge on Larkin. I could tell something bad had happened between the two of them but I didn't push or ask. I just figured this was my opportunity. I told him I wouldn't mind seeing the man dead. Mr Evans said he had a plan, but that it would take a while and some work on my part.

"He told me about an opening for a personal chef for Larkin, that he would pull some strings and get me the job. Then I should just wait and we'd talk later.

"The next time we did talk, it'd been nearly a year. He asked me if I found out anything interesting, and I told him about the peanut allergy. So he came up with the plan. He'd give me the peanut flour that I'd never be able to afford, and I would wait until he was out of town before finding a way to slip it into Larkin's food.

"Chris," Evans said, and his voice was panicked, "stop talking. I mean it."

But Chris was still going, already too deep into the story to dig himself out. "When he texted me that he was out of town, I'd heard Larkin planning on going to Sam's restaurant on my day off. I figured it was the perfect opportunity. I knew enough about their feud to decide to frame him. Before I left for the day, I stole his EpiPen from Mrs Larkin's purse."

"Which you then put in Mrs Larkin's desk?" Tom asked. Chris nodded. "How?"

"Window," Chris said, shrugging. And Maggie remembered Peter talking about the time Chris was looking in all the windows. He'd just been seeing if Mrs Larkin's office windows had been open.

Eyes blazing with a fury Maggie wouldn't have imagined possible from the mild-mannered, Evans stormed toward Chris, arm outstretched.

"Stop. Talking." Evans roared. "Stop talking you fool."

He looked as though he might hit Chris. But before he could, his lawyer intervened, racing forward and grabbing Evans, pulling him away. Everyone stared for a long, uncomfortable minute, disbelief showing on everyone's face at the outburst.

"So you went to Surfer's Point," Tom finally said, drawing the attention back onto Chris. "Was that part of the plan or coincidence?"

"Coincidence," Chris said. "I knew Larkin wouldn't get to the restaurant until noon, so I had time to kill. When I saw Sam there, I realised I needed to wait until he left."

Tom nodded.

Maggie looked over at Evans. His jaw was clenched and his fingers had curled into fists, but his eyes were those of a defeated man.

"And that's pretty much it," Chris said.

"You're an idiot," Evans said. The friendly, mild-mannered man she had first met in The Book Nook was now nowhere to be seen. She would never have thought he would have been capable of murder, but now she knew that a murderer was standing before her. "You're an absolute idiot."

"Constable," Tom said. "I'd appreciate it if you arrested Mr Evans for me."

"Yes, sir." Matthew pulled out his handcuffs and strolled over to Evans and began reciting his rights to him.

Chris waited patiently while Tom approached him and did the same, seemingly resigned to his fate. His eyes were hard and unrepentant, and it was clear that he didn't regret a thing. Maggie followed the five men: two cops, one lawyer, and two men in handcuffs, out of the parlour, through the halls and out into the driveway. The others followed suit. Most were dumbfounded. Mrs Larkin, however, was issuing a vitriolic stream of swear words with every step, though who they were directed at, Maggie wasn't sure.

"Well," Tom said to Maggie, after putting Evans inside the back of the police car. "Is that everything you hoped it would be?"

"It would have been better with a Belgian accent," Maggie said.

"A Belgian accent?" he asked.

"You know, like Poirot."

Tom's eyes sparkled, as he smiled at Maggie.

"There's always next time," he said.

Chapter Twenty-Two

"I KNEW IT WAS HIM," Helena said. "I just had one of those feelings, you know?"

"Come off it, Helena," Bert said, rolling his eyes as he took a sip of beer. "There's no way you had a feeling. You would've gone on about it for ages."

"Maybe I just wanted everyone else to enjoy the mystery," Helena said.

"I'm just glad that it's all sorted out," Liv said, giving Sam a quick peck on the cheek. "Now that the nightmare is finally over, business is coming back. Things are finally getting back to normal. Oh, by the way, did I tell you that I heard that Cadan Anderson and Jenny Tomlin were seen out behind the Smuggler's Inn together? I thought Cadan was supposed to be with Evie."

Maggie zoned out as Liv continued on with her gossip, looking out at the crowded beach from where she sat on the terrace.

The MBC were all relaxing at Sam's restaurant, The Lively Catch, which Sam had closed in a bit of celebration now that everything was over. It was a perfect day for a party, and everyone was enjoying themselves, sipping beer and eating the fish and chips Sam cooked up.

"One of these days you're going to tell me what's in these, mate," Bert said. "You can't keep it a secret forever." He popped a chip into his mouth.

"I'll keep it as long as I can," Sam said, grinning. "I can't have you opening a rival restaurant now, can I?"

"Please," Bert snorted into his beer. "I'd close in a week."

"Have you heard anything from Tom about what's going to happen next?" Kate asked Maggie. The younger girl was still annoyed with her for not taking her along to the Larkin manor, but she was at least putting up a decent front.

"I figure it's best not to pester Tom too much right now, all things considered," Maggie said. "If he wants to tell me anything, he will."

Kate made a face, but didn't argue.

Things were looking up on the whole. June and Jim had warmed back up substantially to Maggie and Kate, and Kate was on the hunt for another job. She was talking about an animal shelter in the next town, and a nearby gym, though Maggie wasn't sure if she would apply for either.

"I did hear that Amélie packed up and left Sandy Cove already," Liv said, overhearing Kate's question and jumping at the new chance for gossip. "And that she's putting the house on the market. Marissa was talking about it while I was doing her hair."

"Do you think she'll get arrested for helping her husband with the lawsuits?" Maggie asked.

"It's possible," Jim said. "But she can always claim she didn't know what Joseph was doing. Her lawyer should be able to get her off without too much effort. But that's not our problem."

"You're right," a voice came from behind Maggie. "It's ours."

Maggie turned to see Tom and Matthew walking toward them.

"Glad you could make it," Sam said, standing and shaking the officers' hands.

"Was a bit surprised by the invitation," Tom said. "I figured you wouldn't want much to do with us considering I thought you might have murdered a man."

"Water under the bridge," Sam said. "And besides, you guys solved the case. You deserve to celebrate too."

"You're too kind." Tom looked over and smiled at Jim. "Doing all right?" he asked.

"Can't complain," Jim said. "Sounds like you boys have your hands full down at the station."

"That's a nice way of putting it," Tom said. "But we'll manage. It's nice to have a day off, though."

"Want a beer?" Bert asked, who was far friendlier to Tom now that Sam was no longer under suspicion.

"That sounds great, actually."

"Well then, help yourself."

The small party continued with more beer and some of Maggie's biscuits that she had brought. People organically broke off into smaller groups and began their own conversations: Kate, Helena, and Bert sat off in one corner; Liv and June leaned up against the railing; Maggie and Tom standing by the table; and Matthew crouched on the ground, preoccupied with his best four-legged friend.

"I swear she likes you more than she likes me," Maggie said, watching Biscuit wriggle happily, hopping up on Matthew and getting sand on his jeans.

"Nah, I'm just the nice man who gives her biscuits, aren't I, girl?" Matthew plucked a biscuit from a plate on the table and held it out for the Cavapoo, who snatched it and chomped it down eagerly.

"Speaking of biscuits," Tom said, glancing over at Maggie. "I heard an interesting rumour the other day about you and Sweet Treats. Any truth to that?"

"You're the detective," Maggie said. "Shouldn't you already know?"

"I prefer to hear it from the source," Tom said. "Otherwise, things get a bit exaggerated. For example, the story I heard is that you fought a dragon, saved Abigail's shop, and she was so grateful to you that she gave you the keys."

Maggie laughed. "That is a tad exaggerated."

"She didn't give you the entire shop? Seems a bit unfair, considering you saved her life from that dragon."

"No dragons," Maggie said. "And no full ownership. Just making biscuits for her a few times a week."

"Seems fitting for you, regardless."

Maggie snapped her fingers. "That reminds me," she said. "Close your eyes."

"What?"

"Just close your eyes and hold out your hand."

He obeyed. Smiling widely, Maggie reached over to the table, picked up a biscuit, and placed it in his outstretched palm. "Okay, you can open them now."

Tom did, and found himself holding a rectangular, golden biscuit.

"Shortbread?" he asked, raising an eyebrow.

"That's your favourite biscuit, isn't it?" Maggie asked. "Did I guess correctly?"

Tom didn't answer immediately. Instead, he just smirked and put the whole thing in his mouth. He closed his eyes, savouring the taste.

"You got it right," he said. "I've been addicted to these since I was a kid."

Maggie's grin grew broader. "It's Biscuit's favourite, too."

"Well then," Tom said, glancing over at the dog. "She has good taste. And she lucked out in terms of her owner. These are excellent."

Reaching over to the plate, Tom grabbed another, chewing thoughtfully.

"So, what now?" Tom asked, swallowing. "Are you giving up The Book Nook?"

"Not quite," Maggie said, glancing over at June. "If things go well with Abigail, then maybe. But I'm not quite ready to say goodbye just yet."

"Understandable," Tom said. "It's a nice place. But if you end up going into baking, I promise you'll have at least one customer."

"I don't think Biscuit counts," Maggie said, hoping that the blush creeping up her face wasn't as noticeable as it felt.

"I was talking about Matthew," Tom said. "He won't quit talking about those hobnobs."

"The bourbons are my favourite," Matthew said.

"There you go," Tom said, smirking. "You'll be in good shape."

"I'll keep that in mind," Maggie said.

"Oi, you two," Bert called. "Need the detective to settle a dispute."

"And what's that?" Tom asked.

"If someone drowns a bloke without wearing gloves, is it going to leave fingerprints?" Bert asked. "I say it will, but Helena thinks it won't, and Kate won't tie-break."

Tom chuckled. "Duty calls," he said, taking a sip of his beer and walking over to the group. "Is it running water or stagnant?" he asked.

Maggie smiled, watching the tableau and enjoying the calm of the warm day and the sounds of the beach nearby. Then she picked up a piece of shortbread, bit into it, and went to join the conversation.

~~~

Free Prequel

Use the QR Code, if you would like a free copy of the Prequel to the Sandy Cove British Mystery series, *Puppy Farm Peril*. It tells the story of how Maggie and her dog, Biscuit met.

Puppy Farm Peril

Pre-order Book 2

Use the QR Code to pre-order your copy of Book 2 in the Sandy Cove British Mystery series, *Vanishing Vows*.

Vanishing Vows

Did you enjoy this book?

If you liked *Deep-Fried Deception,* please leave a rating or write a review so others can discover Siena Summer and the Sandy Cove British Mysteries. Siena loves to receive feedback from her readers.

This QR Code will take you to Siena's sales page, where you can leave a review or rating.

https://bit.ly/Buy_Deep-Fried_Deception

Alternatively, you can leave a review on **Goodreads**

About Siena Summer

SIENA SUMMER HAS ALWAYS loved reading and watching mysteries. Her earliest memories involved watching Scooby-Doo cartoons with her sister. She became a primary (elementary) school teacher and, taught for over 30 years, and always believed there was no greater gift you could give a child than a love of books. Teaching children how to write stories became a genuine passion.

Siena always wanted to write professionally, and finally, her dream is coming true. She is already writing more books for the Sandy Cove British Mystery series. She has fallen in love with her characters and wants to continue writing mysteries for them.

Siena lives in a coastal town in New South Wales, Australia, with her husband and fur kids. Beautiful beaches, bays and national parks surround her and she enjoys the laid-back lifestyle. Siena has two cats

(Felix and Ruby), and a Cavoodle (Cavapoo), named Lily. Siena's dog was the inspiration for the character of Biscuit. They are identical in both looks and personality, right down to their insatiable appetite for biscuits (cookies), especially shortbread.

Follow Siena Summer

Visit Siena Summer's Website:

https://siena-summer-mysteries.mailerpage.io

Keep up-to-date with news, upcoming books, new releases, sales and giveaways. You can also learn more about Sandy Cove and the characters in Siena Summer's books. If you are like Maggie, and like to bake, there are more biscuit recipes from the books on the website.

Siena would love to stay in touch with her readers.

Consider joining Siena Summer's newsletter for news about upcoming books, giveaways and more. You can sign up on her website.

Social Media

Follow Siena on Facebook and Instagram. Use the QR Codes.

Facebook

Instagram

Recipes

CORNISH FAIRINGS

(a spiced ginger biscuit)

Makes 18 biscuits

Ingredients

225g (1 US cup) all-purpose flour

110g (1/2 US cup) caster sugar (granulated)

4 tablespoons golden syrup (light treacle)

1 teaspoon ground cinnamon

3 teaspoons ground ginger

1 teaspoon mixed spice

2 teaspoons baking powder

2 teaspoons bicarbonate of soda (baking soda)

½ teaspoon salt

110g (1/2 US cup) butter

Instructions

1. Preheat the oven to 200 C /180 C Fan/ 400 F

2. Put the dry ingredients, except the sugar, in a large mixing bowl. Mix the spices and flour together thoroughly.

3. Put the butter, sugar and golden syrup in a saucepan over a

medium heat. Stir with a wooden spoon until the mixture has melted.

4. Pour the mixture into the dry ingredients and stir to combine.

5. Divide the dough into 18 balls and place 6 on a lined tray/baking sheet. Place them 10cm (3 inches) apart to allow them to spread. Use the back of a fork to flatten the biscuit slightly.

6. Bake for 8-10 minutes until golden brown.

7. Leave them to cool on the baking tray/sheet for 2 minutes and then transfer to a wire rack to cool completely.

***

Maggie's Shortbread

Makes 30 biscuits

Ingredients

225g (1 US cup) unsalted butter, at room temperature

¾ cup icing/confectioner's sugar

1-2 teaspoons vanilla extract

¼ teaspoon salt

2 ½ cups all-purpose flour

Optional

½ cup chopped dried fruit (cranberries, apricots…)

1/3 cup chopped nuts (pistachios, almonds …)

1 tablespoon fresh zest (orange or lemon)

Instructions

1. In a stand mixing bowl combine the butter and icing/confectioner's sugar and beat on medium speed until the mixture turns light and fluffy, for 3-5 minutes.

2. Add vanilla extract and salt and beat for a further minute.

3. Add the flour in batches and mix on low speed until just combined.

4. At this stage if you are adding fruit, nuts or zest, fold it in using a spatula.

5. Divide the dough into two equal portions. Shape each portion into a log, approximately 18cm long x 5cm wide (7 x 2 inches). Wrap each log in cling wrap or plastic wrap, separately.

6. Refrigerate the dough for at least one hour minimum or overnight.

7. Preheat the oven to 160 C (325 F). Line a baking tray/sheet and set it aside.

8. When it's time to bake, remove the cling/plastic wrap from the log and cut it into slices (about 8mm or 1/3 inch thick).

9. Place them on the prepared baking tray/sheet and bake for 10-12 minutes until the edges start to turn golden.

10. Once done, allow to cool on the tray/baking sheet before transferring to a wire rack, to cool completely.

Note: The dough can be refrigerated for up to one week and frozen for up to 2 months.

***

Homemade Wagon Wheels

Makes 14 biscuits

While you can make these biscuits from scratch, they are a bit fiddly, so here is an easier way to make them. Wagon wheels are a type of sandwich biscuit. Sandwiched between two shortbread biscuits are marshmallow and jam. Then, you dip the biscuit in dark chocolate. This is a very sweet biscuit, so 70% dark chocolate is better.

Ingredients

28 Plain Digestive biscuits (or any round shortbread biscuits)
28 vanilla marshmallows
¼ cup of raspberry jam
375g (13 oz) dark chocolate (70% cocoa)
1 tablespoon of vegetable oil

Instructions

1. Preheat the oven to 160C. Place half the biscuits upside down on a baking tray. Cut each marshmallow if half, then press four halves onto each biscuit. Bake for two minutes, or until the marshmallow is soft and slightly melted. Remove from the oven and set aside for one minute.

2. Spread the jam over the base of the remaining biscuits. Sandwich together each jam biscuit with a marshmallow biscuit, squeezing gently to ensure they stick. Allow to set for 15 minutes, or until the marshmallow has completely cooled.

3. Melt the chocolate in a heatproof bowl set over a saucepan of just-simmering water. Watch it carefully, stirring frequently, to ensure it doesn't burn. Once melted, stir through the oil.

4. Line up your biscuits, chocolate and a baking tray lined with baking paper. Use two forks to dip each biscuit into the chocolate, making sure to fully cover it. Place the biscuit on the baking sheet to set, then either use a metal spatula to smooth the tops or leave them as are. Allow the biscuits to set completely.

Note:

If you want to remove the seeds from the jam, heat the jam gently, then strain it to remove the seeds.

For more biscuit recipes, visit my website.

https://siena-summer-mysteries.mailerpage.io

Acknowledgements

I would like to thank all the people who have helped me with this book. My sounding boards, Noelle and Craig, my editor Christian, my proofreader Edith and my Beta Readers. Your help and input have been invaluable. Also, the cover designers from 100 Covers for your creativity and patience and beautiful cover design.

I would also like to acknowledge my dog, Lily, who was the inspiration for the character of Biscuit.

A special thank you to my husband, family, and friends for your ongoing support and encouragement.

Printed in Great Britain
by Amazon